"Do I have learning problems, too?" asked Caroline. She always had to butt in on everything.

"As a matter of fact, Mrs. Franklin would like to test you. Especially when we told her you were a late reader," Mom said.

"But I read fine now, so why do I have to go?"

"Just to be sure you don't need some brushup," Dad said.

"What a drag!"

But I could tell she was secretly glad to get some of the same attention. She tried to be upset, but she looked almost happy. Sometimes I hated her.

"Okay, okay," I said. "What happens now?"

"Well, we'll set up a tutoring schedule, and I'm afraid you'll have to stop Hebrew . . ."

"Why?"

"Because reading from left to right is hard enough," said Dad. "And reading from right to left just complicates everything."

"I won't quit! Every single one of my friends is in my class!"

"Adam, honey, you gotta do it," said Josephine.

"I hate this whole thing. I hate it!"

I ran out and slammed the door of my room. I could hear Mom and Dad begin to argue again. Caroline walked down the hall and started singing some brainless song just loud enough so that she knew I could hear.

Pretty soon it got quiet again, and I sat staring out the window at the Hudson River. A big tanker rolled toward upstate New York. I wanted to get on and sail away.

ALSO AVAILABLE IN LAUREL-LEAF BOOKS:

Adam Zigzag

Barbara Barrie

LAUREL-LEAF BOOKS

Published by
Bantam Doubleday Dell Books for Young Readers
a division of
Bantam Doubleday Dell Publishing Group, Inc.
1540 Broadway
New York, New York 10036

The trademark Laurel-Leaf Library® is registered in the U.S. Patent
and Trademark Office.
The trademark Dell® is registered in the U.S. Patent and Trademark
Office.

ISBN: 0-440-21964-7

RL: 5.2

Reprinted by arrangement with Delacorte Press

Printed in the United States of America

January 1996

10 9 8 7 6 5 4 3 2 1

OPM

CAMERON BOOKS
3077 W FLORIDA AVE
HEMET CA
92545-0000

909/925-6477   2019739

****

To Aaron, Jane, *and* Jay

and in memory of
Linda Kirschner,
who changed Aaron's life

I would like to thank Bonnie Beach,
Carla Horowitz, and Dr. Fred Covan
for their help in writing this book.

1

Adam

WHEN I was little, I couldn't learn to read, no matter how hard I tried. And my writing looked like pieces of a broken fishnet. You can't imagine how stupid and useless that makes you feel.

I went to a really nice private school at our synagogue in New York City. In the first grade my friends were sitting on cushions and reading in the corners of the schoolroom. They smiled to themselves and sometimes laughed out loud. I'd pretend to read, but no one noticed I kept the same book for days. Sometimes I couldn't sit still, and I'd just walk out the door and go up and down the staircase or to the gym.

Someone would steer me back. Everyone was very gentle and understanding. Mom and Dad would come for conferences, and we'd meet with the principal and the teachers and discuss my wandering around the halls.

It didn't seem strange to me—I'd walked around at night for years. When I was about three, I'd stand by my parents' bed. They'd wake up and ask, "Adam, what is it?" And I'd say things like, "My nose hurts," or, "I had a bad dream," because I didn't want them to know I was frightened. Why couldn't I sleep like the rest of my family?

Sometimes they'd let me stay until morning, but usually they'd take me back to my room and read to me until I fell asleep. Or Dad would just lie down with his arms around me until we both dozed off. I was tired all the time. Looking back on it now, I bet that was one of the reasons school was so hard.

Our house was crammed with books. Mom's an actress, and she'd always be reading. She could cook dinner with a new script in one hand. You'd think the food would be terrible, but it wasn't, although once she got on an East Indian kick, and we didn't have a normal meal for two years.

Dad produces original musical plays for children. He read scripts and books and *The New York Times* and remembered practically every word. My sister's desk was always loaded with dictionaries and a thesaurus and notepaper. She complained about her homework, but she got it done.

By the time I was in the seventh grade, I had tutors three times a week. I hated going to them. I acted as if I were learning, but I knew I wasn't. I could memorize a lesson by hearing it, but the written words looked like zigzags—you know, those "connect-the-dots" books we did when we were in kindergarten? You draw from point to point until it makes a picture. Only on my papers the "picture" never happened. And I could hardly write my own name. I secretly called myself "Adam Zigzag," but to everyone else I pretended to be very cool.

That was hard to do when I tried to read: in the middle of the page the lines would separate, as if someone were erasing the center. Where had the lines gone? It was like a treasure hunt. The missing words! Step right up and find the missing words! Forget it. What I really wanted to do was find my missing life.

2

Adam

I WAS tested when I was seven. Mom took me to see
some lady who lived in an apartment building on
East Ninety-sixth Street. It seemed like a long jour-
ney across Central Park from our apartment on the
Upper West Side. When we got off the bus, I could
see the East River.

Mrs. Franklin had short, curled-under hair like
the pictures of Prince Valiant in the storybook. I
stopped to think. No—actually she probably looked
more like Prince Valiant's mother.

"You're the Brodys . . . yes? It's so nice to meet
you."

"Thank you," Mom said, and we all shook
hands. "When should I come back for Adam?"

"How about two hours, more or less?"

"What are we going to do for two hours?" I asked.

Mrs. Franklin smiled. "Lots of completely fascinating things, I hope."

"I didn't know it would take so long," I said.

The office was like a toy store. Shelves were filled with books, piled in every direction, and board games were spread out, and there were blocks and pencils and drawing papers. A dart board. Maybe this wouldn't be so bad.

"Adam, would you like some true junk food? Milky Ways, Oreos, Chips Ahoy, or Cocoa Puffs?"

"Nothing, thank you."

"Well, how about some pink lemonade? It's a pretty hot morning."

"Well . . . okay, thanks."

Mrs. Franklin called from the kitchen, "How's the second grade treating you?"

"Okay." I felt a little lonely.

She gave me a tall, cold paper cup. "Do you know why you're here?"

"What?"

"Did your mom or dad tell you why you're here?"

"Oh. To find out what I do best."

"Exactly. What are your favorite subjects?"

"What?"

"What do you enjoy studying?"

"Gym and math. I'm great at math."

"What do you like least?"

"Science."

"I don't hear anything about English."

"I'm not so good at English."

"Do you like school?"

"I don't like my seat. I want to get up all the time."

"I don't blame you. Kids should be able to jump around once in a while, right?"

"Right." Mrs. Franklin was very smart.

She held up a paper with drawings on it. "Will you copy these shapes for me?"

"Okay. But what if I can't?"

"There's no right or wrong on this."

I bent low over the paper, so I could do good work. I worked slowly. It was fun, but not easy.

"Excellent, Adam. Now would you read out loud for me?"

"Well, I . . . uh . . ."

"No pass or fail on this one either. It's just another way to learn about you."

I liked the sound of my voice as I read: it was strong and loud. When I stumbled over a word, Mrs. Franklin helped me.

Sometimes she wrote in her notebook. Was she writing that I didn't read well? Or that I did?

"Just dandy, Adam. How's the lemonade? Need a refill?"

"Yes, please."

Mrs. Franklin went to the kitchen, then came back with a plate of cookies and the lemonade.

"Adam, stand by the window, please, and point to the tallest building."

I pointed to a pink high rise with a swimming pool under a glass dome. "Now," Mrs. Franklin said, "hop on one foot." This was getting silly, and I laughed and hopped in a circle.

"Can you skip?"

I skipped back to the desk and turned around.

"Very good, Adam. Now hold out your hands, close your eyes, and count to twenty."

As I got to twenty, Mrs. Franklin said, "Open your eyes. What do you see?"

"My left arm is below my right."

"You've got it. You're right-handed and right-footed, too."

"What does that mean?"

"Different sides of our brains control certain actions."

"Do I have something wrong with my brain?"

"Not at all. But the more I get to know you, the more I see how everything works."

We played a game of darts. And I won.

"Fantastic! What sports do you like?"

"Basketball."

"What else?"

"I'd like to play tennis, but I'd never be as good as my dad."

"I think you can do anything you want to do. Now will you draw a picture of yourself?"

I drew a squat, bowlegged man with a feather in his belt. And a house with smoke coming from the chimney in puffy, black clouds.

I read a story silently. Then Mrs. Franklin asked

questions: Had I liked it? What was the name of the main character? What had happened to her?

I was getting tired. Mrs. Franklin said, "That's it! We're done. And Adam, I know someone who could help you. She'll help you learn new things. Would you like to meet her?"

"Well, maybe. Can I ask my mom and dad?"

"Of course. And then will you call me?"

"By myself?"

"You don't use the phone?"

"I'm afraid I'll dial wrong."

"No, you won't. Just try it."

She helped me on with my coat. "You have the name of a television show printed on your shirt. It says 'Ben O'Neil, Twentieth Precinct.' "

"That's my mom's show."

"What does 'Twentieth Precinct' mean?"

"What?"

"What do these words mean?"

"I guess it means that they do it twenty times or something."

"Do what twenty times?"

"Oh . . . arrest people or shoot people."

"Find out, will you? And then call me?"

"Okay. Am I through?"

"You are. You're a smart, friendly boy. I hope you know that."

"Thanks."

"We'll keep in touch, Adam."

Mom was waiting for me at the door. All the way home, I wondered, why did I need help if I was so "smart"? There must be something wrong with my brain, no matter what Mrs. Franklin said.

That night I leaned against the window and had a daydream that I was reading two books at a time and making all A's. I wasn't running up and down the stairs at school, and everyone was smiling at me.

3

Adam

Mom opened a thick letter and spread the pages out on the kitchen table.

"Adam, darling, sit down, and we'll explain Mrs. Franklin's report to you."

"Is it bad?"

"Not at all," Dad said. "It clears up a lot of things. We had a long talk with her yesterday."

"I'm really dumb, right?"

They laughed so quickly that I knew they were worried. Parents think they can hide things like that, but they never can.

"You know, I was dyslexic when I was a kid," Mom said. "I still am. They just called it something different in those days."

"They called it 'being dumb,' Mom."

"No, they didn't. I was bright—just like you—and I got a lot of help, and I went to college and everything."

"Listen to this, Adam." Dad held one of the pages and put on his glasses. " 'Dyslexia means difficulty with the symbols of language—letters and numbers. Each child is different. Adam can be tutored so that he can learn in his own way.' "

"Tutored?"

"Don't panic," Dad said.

"Mr. B., go easy on him. This is a lot of stuff at one time, right, hon?" Josephine put her hands on my shoulders. She's our housekeeper. Well, kind of. I mean she does everything for everybody, and bosses us all like crazy while she's doing it. "This boy is going to be fine. You all lower your voices and be nice to each other."

"Why is everybody screaming?" Caroline, my sister, always exaggerates. She fell into one of the chairs and rolled her eyes. "I can't get my homework done."

"Sorry," said Mom. "We're explaining Mrs. Franklin's report to Adam."

"Can he be cured?"

"He can be helped to find words that are in his head," Mom said.

"You mean the ones I always stutter over?" I asked.

Mom and Dad suddenly got very quiet and sorrowful. I felt like a lowlife. It was all my fault.

"Yes," said Mom. "You know lots of words, but

you have a little trouble sometimes forming the *sounds* of the words."

"But how come I can picture a word in my head?"

Daddy looked surprised. "You mean you know you can do that?"

"Sure, I can 'see' it, but I can't get it to come out of my mouth."

"It's called 'dysnomia,' Adam. Lots of people have it. Mrs. Franklin wants us to throw you the words when you need them," said Mom. "I wish I'd had you tested last year, but everyone talked me out of it."

"It does no good to look back," Dad said.

"But now we have to make up for lost time. Why didn't I just follow my instincts? I know what it's like not to be able to read!"

"I don't want to discuss it, Ann!"

"All right, everybody, just get out of my kitchen if you're gonna fight!" Josephine stood over us, her eyes shooting little spikes into the air.

"Sorry, Jo," my dad said. "This is just so new to us . . ."

"Do I have learning problems, too?" asked Caroline. She always had to butt in on everything.

"As a matter of fact, Mrs. Franklin would like to test you. Especially when we told her you were a late reader," Mom said.

"But I read fine now, so why do I have to go?"

"Just to be sure you don't need some brushup," Dad said.

12

"What a drag!"

But I could tell she was secretly glad to get some of the same attention. She tried to be upset, but she looked almost happy. Sometimes I hated her.

"Okay, okay," I said. "What happens now?"

"Well, we'll set up a tutoring schedule, and I'm afraid you'll have to stop Hebrew . . ."

"Why?"

"Because reading from left to right is hard enough," said Dad. "And reading from right to left just complicates everything."

"I won't quit! Every single one of my friends is in my class!"

"Adam, honey, you gotta do it," said Josephine.

"I hate this whole thing. I hate it!"

I ran out and slammed the door of my room. I could hear Mom and Dad begin to argue again. Caroline walked down the hall and started singing some brainless song just loud enough so that she knew I could hear.

Pretty soon it got quiet again, and I sat staring out the window at the Hudson River. A big tanker rolled toward upstate New York. I wanted to get on and sail away.

4

Caroline

I WAS in the fourth grade when they figured out Adam was dyslexic. Everyone ran around to doctors and testers and moaned and groaned about this poor little boy's dreadful affliction.

The worst part of it is that they decided I might have learning problems too. I did read later than almost everyone else in my class. I felt really dumb when my best friends, who were twins, read at night when we had sleep-overs, and I just stared at picture books.

So they dragged me to this Mrs. Franklin, and I was scared that she would find out that I was slow or demented or something. She gave me humungous tests over two days. I hated them, but she let me drink pink lemonade and eat junky cookies, so that helped.

Once she said, "Now, Caroline, you don't have to do this test perfectly."

"If I don't have to do it perfectly, why did you give it to me?" I knew I sounded like a smart-mouth, troubled kid. And here I was trying to appear so normal.

But she didn't get angry, and after she studied my tests, she sent me to Mrs. Hirshey, this wonderful tutor on Central Park West.

The next year I had to take another test, called the Educational Records Bureau . . . the dreaded ERB. It measures how much you know. Or how much they think you should know.

I had to take it because when I graduated from the synagogue school in the sixth grade, all the possible new schools would want to look at the test. If you don't do well on the ERB, some schools won't even consider you.

Mrs. Franklin had ordered one for Adam too. My parents were trying to find a school for him— one that knew how to teach dyslexic kids.

You go to this musty brownstone building and sit on fake leather furniture in a waiting room full of children and their parents. Everyone looks tense. Especially the parents. They try to read, but their eyes dart around the room.

Adam was called first. He waved good-bye as if he were leaving for Europe. We had just come home from summer vacation, and his hair was like a sun-bleached bowl. He looked so cute. What if the test was too hard for him? And for me too?

Daddy read a script, and I tried to finish some

homework. About twenty minutes later, Adam came out, pencil smudges all over his face.

"Daddy, how do you spell 'Brody'?"

My father put down his script. "Say that again, please."

"How do you spell 'Brody'?"

Daddy took Adam's chin in his hand. "Honey, that's your last name."

"I know, but I think I'm spelling it wrong."

"How are you spelling it?"

"Uh . . . B . . . O . . . D . . . R . . . Y."

Daddy took in a little breath. "No, darling, it's B . . . R . . . O . . . D . . . Y."

"It is? I knew I was wrong."

"Do you want me to write it down for you?"

"No, I got it. Thanks, Dad."

He skipped back into the testing room, and I thought Daddy would cry. His face started moving around, and he tried to read again. Finally he just stared out the window.

"Daddy, that's not so terrible," I said. He gave me a little smile.

A woman with glasses hanging around her neck peeked around the corner. "Caroline, we're ready for you."

"You'll be just fine," he said. But I could tell he was still thinking about Adam.

I finished my test early and came out to the waiting room. Where were all the other kids? I was either very smart or very stupid. I would probably be banished to some special school in another state.

Adam finished a few minutes later. He said, "Can we get some ice cream?"

"How did it go?" Daddy asked.

"Great. I drew lots of pictures. Can we get some ice cream?"

"Absolutely," said Daddy. "Shall we go to Rumpelmayer's and get ice cream sundaes for fifty dollars apiece?"

Adam started jumping up and down. "Fifty dollars . . . really?"

"Well, not quite. But they have the best hot fudge in Manhattan."

Daddy is wild about sweet things. And when he's unhappy or nervous, it's sugar, sugar, sugar. So we took a taxi—another unusual treat—to Rumpelmayer's on Central Park South, where the waitresses in their little starched hats and aprons brought us extra cookies and petit fours.

Adam and I couldn't finish our mountains of ice cream. The tall, silver cups perspired and soaked the paper doilies on the saucers, so Daddy ate his and ours. He had chocolate sauce in the corner of his mouth, which is so embarrassing, but we didn't want to tell him.

After all, he was trying his best. But his son couldn't spell his own name, and his daughter might have scored "zero" in everything. His sadness blew across the table like a gray ghost.

5

Adam

"Mom, let's read *Tom Sawyer* tonight."

"You don't want to finish *Alice in Wonderland*, Adam?"

"*Alice* is not for kids. Why do people think it is?"

Mom laughed and gave me a hug. "You have an original mind for a nine year old."

We plumped the pillows and settled down on my bed. The lights of New Jersey across the river made a shiny pattern through the windowpane.

I put my head on Mom's shoulder. Huck Finn and Tom were running away.

"Don't you think, Mom, they were made to be friends?"

"I do. It was 'written in the stars.' "

"I want a friend like that."

"But the fourth grade is full of good kids. And isn't John your best friend?"

"He's a friend. But he's smarter than I am."

"Nonsense!"

"Oh, John and I both know it. I want a gang."

"What?"

"I want a whole bunch of kids who don't care that I can't read or write and . . ."

"But you're getting better every day!"

". . . and who go everywhere with me. And who think I'm great."

"You'll have that, darling."

"Yeah?"

"Of course you will. You're terrific. Anybody would want to be your friend."

She turned out the light and tucked me in. "Now don't worry about it. Sleep well. I'll see you in the morning."

"Mom?"

"Yes, honey?"

"I want . . ."

"Yes?"

"Nothing . . . Good night."

6

Caroline

ALL through the fifth, sixth, and seventh grades I went to my tutor, Mrs. Hirshey. We'd work at her dining room table near the window. You could see the Central Park Reservoir and the tennis courts and the apartment houses lining Fifth Avenue in the distance. In the fall the trees were like a yellow and orange and red blanket with light bulbs glowing underneath.

Mrs. Hirshey had a brother who had always gotten the attention when she was growing up, so she understood how I felt about Adam. We spent lots of time talking about that. Sometimes I think that's why Mrs. Franklin put us together: she knew I would have a sympathetic friend. And I really did.

Actually I was glad to get extra help. After the synagogue school, I got into West Side Prep. It was so hard that I didn't know how I'd survive. My first English assignment was to report on an editorial in *The New York Times* about abortion. I didn't even know what the word meant! Mrs. Hirshey explained it all and helped me write the paper. She brought me way up on math and science, and we spoke only French whenever we could.

When I didn't have to go anymore, I really missed those afternoons. Who could I talk to now? Who would help me with this Adam situation? Everything he did was a major event.

I'll give you an example:

One rainy day, when Adam was in the third grade, he was late getting home from school.

Josephine said, "Caroline, did Adam have choir practice today?"

"He's probably playing video games at the corner."

But I called Fun Unlimited, and the owner said that Adam wasn't there.

At five o'clock Josephine phoned the school. Closed. She called practically every friend of Adam's. At five-thirty little bites of fear began to jab into my side, like a cramp you get after running too hard.

Mom came home from rehearsal at six. "He's lost?" she said. She and Jo put their arms around each other and stood still in the middle of the kitchen.

"I'm going to look for him," Mom said.

"Me too," I said. I didn't want to be left out, even if all this effort was going toward Adam. As usual.

It was starting to rain. Amsterdam Avenue had dead-end alleys and bad-smelling hallways. The city was full of junkies and just plain nut-cases. And it was dark.

The rain was turning to hail. Our shoes squirted water as we waited for the light to change. "Oh, God, just please let him be all right," Mom said.

But no Adam.

Back in the apartment, Josephine said, "Jacob's on the way home. He's calling the police."

"I'll finish the corn bread," Mom said. "You set the table, Caro." The wind and hail were pounding against the kitchen window.

As Mom started to mix the cornmeal, she began to speak slowly. "This is the last thing I'll probably ever cook. I'll add this salt and turn on this oven so that when I'm very old, I'll remember having done it."

A streak of lightning and a bolt of thunder exploded. We all jumped and screamed. The phone rang.

"Hello?" Jo was shouting. "Adam . . . you what? You're *where*?" She put her hand over the receiver. "He says he's at Rob's, across the street. You won't believe this, but he wants to stay for dinner. They're having macaroni and cheese."

"I don't care if they're having caviar and gold bricks!" Mom shouted.

22

Jo turned back to the phone. "You get yourself home, boy. Do you know what time it is? No, it's not five o'clock. It's almost eight!"

We had forgotten that Adam couldn't tell time!

Daddy came dripping rain through the front door.

"He's all right, Jay. He's been at the Justins' all afternoon," Mom said.

"On the subway," said Daddy, taking off his coat, "I prayed that if only he were safe, I'd never ask him to do another reading exercise."

"He's safe, thanks be to Jesus," Jo said.

"I swore that I'd let him go to the movies for the rest of his life," said Mom, who was crying and laughing at the same time. "Now he'll be lucky if I ever let him out of the house again!"

"How about me?" I asked. "Can I go to movies for the rest of my life? Or would you like to put me into foster care?"

Daddy kissed me. "You may see two films every day from now until you are ninety-two."

The front door opened.

"Well, here I am," said Adam, dropping his sneakers into a puddle on the rug. "What's for dinner?"

So you see, that's how it was most of the time. It was as if no one knew I was in the house. I did my work and made my bed and put my dirty clothes into the hamper.

Meanwhile Mom and Dad were in Adam's room for hours practically every evening, doing his homework and waking him up every morning.

I turned off my alarm, took my shower, and went to the kitchen for breakfast. He'd come in with his shirt hanging out and his sneakers unlaced. Everyone would fuss over his food and make him drink his juice. They'd gather up all his books and papers; and there I was, with the perfect ponytail which I had fixed myself.

I guess they figured I was older and more responsible, and no one said, "How'ya doing?" or anything like that. When I got to school, my voice felt rusty and unused.

Adam had guitar teachers and piano teachers, and he went from one tutor to another. There were always meetings with the principal and psychologist and hundreds of phone conversations. Home was a very unpeaceful place. So I stayed in my room.

You know that kids' poem, "Oh, my goodness, what a shame, there goes Alice down the drain?" Well, that was me, folks. That was absolutely me.

7

Caroline

WHEN I was twelve years old, I wore oversized men's coats. Everyone thought I was slightly cuckoo, but then big, loose clothes became really "in." So I was a little before my time, if I do say so myself.

I begged the coats from my father and my Uncle Melvin, who sent me his from Chicago. They were soft and old, and Mom had new silk linings put into them. I saved my allowance and began collecting watches too.

Mom loved to shop with me. "You know about shapes of clothes and lengths of earrings and the variations of the lowly bandanna—boy, do I admire you!" She always asked me what to wear for meetings and things.

"What do you want for your birthday, Caroline?" Dad asked.

"I don't know, but could we go on a 'looking tour'?"

"Perfect," said Mom. "I have to buy graduation presents. Let's spend next Sunday together, darling."

"Okay, Mom. But please don't wear your funny clothes and bracelets."

"How about a plain skirt and sweater?"

"Great."

I knew she wanted "special time" with me because in those days they were completely taken up with Adam's problems. But once in a while—I hate to say this—I think they felt guilty. And suddenly we would go to a museum or on "marathon movie days" or shopping trips.

And the lunch possibilities were endless: salads on upper Broadway, Mexican food in Hell's Kitchen, Indian pakoras and dosas in Greenwich Village. That was really fun because I loved to eat everything!

This day we were eating hot dogs, sauerkraut, and spicy pickles on the Lower East Side in a famous, noisy kosher delicatessen. I looked into her shopping bag.

"Mom, this material would be great to line that old skirt of yours."

"Oh, am I giving you that skirt?"

"Yes, but you didn't know it."

"When was this decision made?"

26

"When I saw this silk. The pattern is incredible."

"Well, maybe, but don't say I never did anything for you, Caroline."

"It would make up for your missing *The Wizard of Oz*."

"When you were in the fourth grade?"

"Yes, you were in California."

"I beg your pardon. I finished my performance at the theater, caught a 'red-eye' flight, flew all night to Kennedy Airport, and came right to the school."

"Oh, really, Mommy?" I said, wide-eyed.

"You played 'The Lion,' and I heard every adorable roar."

"Are you sure?"

"Daddy and I came backstage and told you how wonderful you were. Then I took a cab back to Kennedy, flew all day, went to the theater in Los Angeles, and did another performance! You little devil, you remember perfectly."

I leaned over and kissed her. "I've always loved that story."

"I know. But darling, sometimes late at night, or when I'm doing the laundry, I think maybe I could have been a better mother—the kind who leads the Girl Scout troop and is home and asks, 'How was your day?'"

"No, Mom, you had to do 'your thing.' We all knew that." I was suddenly shy. "Anyway, it's kind of cool to have a mother who acts."

27

"The trouble with acting is that it's so irregular —lots of work one month, then none for the next seven."

"I know that, Mom."

"So actors have to go where the work is. We have lots of bills to pay, darling. . . ."

"It's okay. I really understand."

"But you've been lonely a lot, haven't you?"

I looked down. "Well, sometimes."

"Oh, Caroline, I'll try and make it up to you."

"How about giving me that skirt?"

"Opportunist!"

"You bet!"

"Even so, Caroline, you are the daughter of my dreams."

I grinned. "Don't get gushy, Mom."

8

Adam

By the end of sixth grade, I could read and write just enough to get by. All my friends could do things "Adam Zigzag" couldn't even attempt, but I tried not to think about it, even though I was graduating from the synagogue school and had to look for another place.

I took a tour of Caroline's school, West Side Prep, and it was awesome—really "grown-up," busy, lots of laughter, good food in the cafeteria. I knew I wanted to go there.

"Adam, it's such a hard school," said Mom. "Why not choose one that's more flexible?"

"I can do the work!"

"Adam, it's a total grind," said Caroline.

"Why are you all picking on me?"

"Because we want you to be in an atmosphere that encourages you," said Dad. "West Side is not the place for you."

"Why don't you give me a chance!"

So Mom and Dad met with the admissions department, and two weeks later I had an interview, and then we were all invited for a meeting. So far I had won!

As we walked down the hall, kids were rushing from class to class, some from swimming practice, their hair still wet, book bags hanging on one shoulder.

They wore torn blue jeans and sweatshirts that said "Greenpeace," or "Save the Dolphins," or "Pro-Choice." They seemed happy.

I wanted to be like that—I was sick of being someone everyone else worried about. I could make it if only they'd let me try!

The headmaster, Mr. French, said, "Adam, how do you think you'd do here?" I was sitting on a cracked leather couch in his office. There were basketball and swimming trophies on all the shelves. Books and papers everywhere.

I had to do something if I was going to get into this school. I thought fast.

"Did you know, Mr. French, that next year you may have the most talented, short player in New York City on your basketball team?"

"You're going to try out for the team? Well . . ."

"Don't worry. I'm pretty good, and in September I'll have grown a few hundred inches."

"We hope you'll go for everything, Adam. We also have an extensive music program, and I hear you sing and play the guitar."

"I do. And I'm beginning to compose now." Which was true, but it sounded phony when I said it. I thought I'd better shut up. Didn't want to be too eager.

"Mr. French . . . uh . . ." Mom looked embarrassed.

"Yes?"

She looked at me and then at Dad.

"We think Adam might be happier . . ."

"Yes, Mrs. Brody?"

Now Dad began sputtering. "Well, at a less-structured school perhaps. If you remember, at our first meeting, we told you that Adam . . ."

I hated it when they spoke for me like that, as if I didn't have a thought of my own. As if I weren't even in the room. Were they afraid to say "learning problems"? Did they think they couldn't tell the truth in front of me?

"What do *you* think, Adam?" Mr. French asked.

"I want to be here. This is really the place for me . . . more than any other school I've seen."

"Adam has a bar mitzvah in about a year," said Mom.

31

"But not until the eighth grade. I can handle that."

"The seventh grade will be a busy year for you," said Mr. French. "You'll have to organize the work."

"It's not so simple," Mom said. "He has tutoring and it takes Adam"—another glance in my direction—"a little longer to do things."

"We have people who are equipped to help him. In time Adam won't need tutors at all."

"It sounds a little too easy," said Dad.

"Not at all, Mr. Brody. Anything else you'd like to know, Adam?"

"No, thanks, sir." I smiled what I hoped was my most dazzling smile.

"You're going to love it here." He stood up and held out his hand. "Trust me."

Walking home, Mom and Dad took my hands. I felt protected. I would succeed next year! I would be in the right school, no matter what they thought! At West Side Prep there would be teachers who understood my dyslexia and would help me learn all the things that had been such mysteries.

No more "Adam Zigzag," because I would read and write like everyone else. Even do math! The jittery numbers would finally make sense.

And now I'd have a "gang." Maybe be on an athletic team. If basketball didn't work out (I was a seriously short person), maybe I'd try for swimming.

West Side Preparatory School would be the best thing that ever happened to me.

9

Caroline

By the ninth grade, the West Side Prep girls' volley-ball team was the great part of my life. We traveled all over to play other schools. We sang in the bus coming home, all sweaty and happy. Except, of course, when we lost. But that wasn't too often.

And schoolwork was getting easier. Still it took me twice as long to do homework as it did anyone else. That's why sometimes I felt sorry for Adam. I knew what it felt like to be afraid all the time. And to feel everyone was smarter.

When Adam came to West Side Prep, I was speaking French and learning about the Impressionists and making pottery and using watercolor in art class.

I liked a boy, Jonathan Guettel, but none of us

really dated. We just kind of hung out at parties and on weekends at the movies on Broadway. We did homework together. We went to pizza parlors after athletic practice, and sometimes the girls went shopping in Greenwich Village or on Columbus Avenue. My allowance was usually almost gone, so I could only afford a pair of dollar earrings or a notepad, but that was fun anyhow.

But the school was small. Some of my oldest friends went to Darby, another school across town, and I was getting up my nerve to ask my parents if I could apply there.

And then Adam enrolled. Suddenly here comes this blond, angelic boy. "Oh, he's so cute!" everyone said. No one had to tell me I was definitely not "cute." No cheekbones. Too skinny. A gigantic nose.

Adam winged through the halls like a little airplane. Talking and waving and smiling. People always gathered around him, but he was so short that he disappeared into the cluster of blue jeans and book bags and ponytails.

He was invited to parties and Broadway plays and weekends at his friends' country homes. I could tell Mom and Dad were thrilled that he was so popular.

He went skiing in Vermont and apple picking in upstate New York. At Christmas he went to Barbados with Suzanne Bear, and her parents paid for the whole thing—even the airplane ticket! It was so quiet then, almost as if I were an only child. I wasn't sure I liked that, but I wouldn't have admitted it to anyone.

His friends came over to study with him. They all sat around the room discussing social studies or Shakespearean plays. They wrote their papers together. They'd drill him on spelling. They'd coach him on geometry and history. Loudly. I could hear every word through my door. Sometimes I'd yell, "Shut up!" or sit in the kitchen to do my homework.

Jo would say, "Baby, it's noisy back there!"

"It's like living in the middle of an MTV video, Josephine."

"I know, honey, but he needs all the help he can get."

But even with all the attention, West Side was just too hard for him. I knew it would be.

Sometimes I'd think about how much I'd loved him when he was little. I walked him to school every day. He held my hand tightly as we passed through the rough blocks. He thought I was perfect, and I was so proud of him.

"Adam, what color is the light?" I'd ask.

"It'th yellow." He spoke with this adorable lisp.

"Do we cross on the yellow, Adam?"

"No, Caro. We have to wait for the green."

"What would happen if we went too soon?"

"Too thoon? It would be dangerouth."

He was so trusting and sweet. I wanted to protect him forever.

10

Adam

As soon as I came to West Side Prep, Caroline began to get angry at me all the time. She said I was loud and lazy. When I started bumming out in my classes, she didn't offer to help or anything.

I tried to keep up, but math was so hard it made my head ache. In English class, the words were flying off the pages and into the air.

My notebooks were empty because I couldn't figure out the margins. My vocabulary was like the Invisible Shrinking Man, and my handwriting looked like broken Pick-Up Sticks.

By March, I was talking back to the teachers and sleeping too much and not showing up for my tutors. Caroline said I was embarrassing her, but I couldn't stop. I wanted her to be my sister again, to be proud of me the way she was when I was little, but I'd pass her in the halls, and she'd barely say hello.

I was just beginning to prepare for my bar mitzvah, and it was scary. I had crazy dreams at night that I'd forget everything and stand there like a coatrack. Caroline's bas mitzvah had been perfect. She'd been a star. I wanted to talk to her about it, but she barely acknowledged that I was alive.

I loved Caroline a lot. She'd protected me from rough kids. She'd bought me ice cream after school, and we'd looked in shop windows and ridden our bikes in Riverside Park.

When I was six, she was my best friend. One day she put her arm around me and gave me a squeeze. She said, "All my friends want a brother like you."

It was the last nice thing she said to me for years and years.

11

Adam

DAD and I would review the assignment.

We'd get out the paper. I could feel myself get too quiet. I'd put my head down and bang a ruler against my leg. Or roll a pen back and forth.

I needed a bathroom break. Dad would go into the living room and open a script. A half hour—no sound. Back down the hall came Dad, and I'd be lying on my bed, staring up at the ceiling.

"Adam, honey, let's get going."

"Dad, I'm really worried about my bar mitzvah."

"Can we talk about this later?"

"I mean, since I can't take Hebrew anymore, isn't it kind of lying to pretend that I'm really reading it on the Big Day?"

"Adam, most people memorize their portion of

the Torah anyway. It's what's in your heart that matters, not whether or not you really can read Hebrew."

"But what if I fall on my face?"

"You won't. You'll be thoroughly rehearsed by then. Think of people who are denied a bar mitzvah . . ."

"Who?"

"Citizens of the Soviet Union . . ."

"Russia?"

"Yes."

"What would happen if they had one anyway?"

"They'd suffer terrible discrimination—in jobs, housing, advancement in their fields, acceptance at certain schools . . ."

"That's pretty bad."

"To say the very least. But the day of your bar mitzvah you'll be joyously accepted as . . ."

"I know, 'an adult member of the Jewish Community.' "

"Yep, a privilege. Now come on, let's get back to the lesson."

"Okay, I'm ready, Freddy." I'd arrange the paper and adjust the swivel chair. Five more minutes. "Shoot, Dad."

"Is this play a comedy or a drama?"

"A drama."

"Good. Why, Adam?"

"Because . . . because . . . it's about a father who thinks he's a failure, and how miserable his family becomes."

"Right!"

"So what do I do now?"

"What's the assignment, son?"

"To explain the plot and my . . . Dad, what's the word for what I think of something?"

"Your reaction?"

"No."

"Opinion?"

"No, Mr. Brody, but you're getting closer. Would you like to try for the grand sweepstakes?"

"How about 'evaluation'?"

"That's it, audience! Mr. Brody has won the Jamaica vacation *and* a new car."

Then I wanted a sandwich and hot chocolate. It got to be eleven o'clock, and I didn't want to admit how tired—and worried—I was. These assignments made no sense unless someone helped me.

We went back to my room. "Will you show me where to start the paragraph?"

I couldn't "see" a block of handwriting centered in a blank space, so Dad showed me the lefthand corner of the paper. I traveled down a few lines with my finger. I focused on that spot like a pilot coming in for a landing.

But I'd grip the pen too hard, and the point would separate into two useless pieces.

Change to ballpoint. No ink. Dad sighed.

"Dad, are you angry at me?"

"No, not at all." But he was.

Now I wanted ice water. Into the kitchen. We carried the pitcher and glasses back to my room.

And then the new pen went bonkers. Search for another.

It was almost midnight. Sleep was creeping up from my ankles. Dad put a sheet of paper into the typewriter; and while I dictated, he finished the assignment.

"Do you understand why the theme of this play is relevant?"

"Revelant?"

"No, rel-a-vant."

"Re-l-avant."

"Right. Could families behave this way today?"

"Yes."

"You bet. Great writers' work just gets better with time. Now let's get ourselves to bed."

"Thanks for helping me, Dad." He looked exhausted. We pretended that he hadn't done most of the work.

I brushed my teeth and got into bed. Dad turned out the light and lay down beside me.

"You know when you were a baby, I took your three o'clock feeding."

"How come?"

"Mommy was in a Broadway show, and she would have just wound down and gone to bed. Besides, I wanted to. I'd hold you—hungry and crying—and I'd say, 'Wait, kid, stop wailing, can't you see the milk is almost ready?' "

"What would I do?"

"You'd either get quiet or cry harder."

"Poor Dad."

"No, lucky Dad. You'd put your arms around my neck and we'd look over the rooftops of Manhattan together. I'd wonder if I was the only wide-awake adult in the city. And if I'd ever again get to sleep through an entire night."

"Was it awful?"

"Looking back on it, it was wonderful. We'd sit in the rocking chair while you drank, and your handsome eyes would stare steadily at me. Sometimes you'd pull away and smile, an astonishingly sweet and happy smile."

"Tell me more."

"I'd laugh and kiss you. I'd talk. Sometimes sing a little song. You'd gurgle back, and often we'd both fall asleep, the bottle still in my hand when the sun came into the kitchen."

He put his arm around me and snored slightly.

"Dad, will you stay till I fall asleep?"

"Like old times?"

"Yeah, like old times."

"Close your eyes, honey. I'll stay."

And we slept.

12

Adam

"Sunder everything we love in slave maner means to separate our famales, To put our kids on boats and sell them there. It means to wip our relitifes in frount of us and not beaing able to help them. (and sufering) This is an example, One man and his wife and children, were on pla a plantation picking cotton and when they wre done for the day, the man and the children were in a room listining to there mouther and wife being whiped in the outher room. And they coden codentl do anything. (CAN YOU EMAGING THAT HAPPING TO YOU THATS SAD)"

"You know your subject, Adam. And you have a specific emotional response to it." Mrs. Franklin put my essay into a folder.

"I wish I could have written it better . . . you know, the right punctuation and all."

"Just keep working."

"I don't want any more tutors."

"But you want to be a better writer."

"I can't go to any more tutors! I've been doing this since the second grade! Five years!"

"How do the teachers at West Side Prep treat you?"

I bent down to my shoelace and then swiveled around on the chair. "They make me feel . . ."

"They make you feel what, Adam?"

"Dumb! They make me feel like a criminal or something! They say I'm lazy and . . ." I was trying not to bawl.

"But you know you're not any of those things."

"Who says?"

"Your sharp mind says it. And I say it. But I think we should look for another school."

"Those dumps have dummies in them. I won't go!"

"I know of a wonderful school that has great kids, just like you, where the pressure isn't so terrible."

"It doesn't matter what school I go to. If I can't do seventh-grade work, and I'm twelve years old . . . I'm never gonna get it!"

Mrs. Franklin walked around her desk and put her hand on my head. "You are 'gonna get it,' Adam. But either it's tutors or a new school. Let's get real."

I hate it when grown-ups talk like that—as if they're trying to be just like you. "Why doesn't everyone just leave me alone?"

"Because we want you to be happy, Adam."

"I'm never gonna be happy!"

"And we want you to be successful. We've got to make some quick moves."

"I'm gonna move right outa town."

"No, I'll see you next week. I promise you things will get better."

I pounded out of that office. I'd quit school. I'd run away. I'd jump into the East River. Because I wasn't going to do any of this stuff anymore.

13

Caroline

My mother wanted a brass bed.

"There's a place on the Lower East Side where they display all the hardware, and you design your own bed," she said.

Daddy clutched his head and made a face. "Ann, we have the bar mitzvah coming up. We don't need to spend a lot of money."

"It won't be expensive. This is like a big junk warehouse. You just wander around by yourself."

We all piled in our beat-up station wagon. On Orchard Street we climbed five flights, Daddy and Adam complaining all the while. Suddenly we were in this huge loft, with sunlight spilling through two skylights.

Leaning against the walls and strewn across the

floor were hundreds of brass or wrought-iron rails, bed frames, headboards, knobs, and finials. There were decorations—angels, houses, flowers—some old, some shiny new.

A big man in a long, black coat and furry hat walked through this sea of metal. His beard curled out in every direction. His black lace-up shoes looked like boats.

"Good day. I am Chaim Levin. Ask me anything you like. We will lengthen a piece of brass, or shorten it, or make an extra large bed." He had a thick accent, maybe Polish or Russian, I couldn't tell. "And you can design your headboard using any of the elements you see."

Mom was in heaven. Daddy looked bored and started meandering around. Adam stared at the big man in the black coat.

"Is something wrong, young man?"

"No, sir . . . it's your hat . . . is it . . . ?"

"It's beaver," said Mr. Levin. "A Jew must always have his head covered, you know. Would you like to see it?"

"Yes, thanks," said Adam.

"Try it on," he said and handed it to Adam.

It fell down over his nose. All you could see was his mouth and chin and this enormous black hat.

Daddy laughed. Mom turned around, with a brass bouquet in her hand, and said, "Adam, that's the kind of hat my grandfather wore."

Mr. Levin looked interested. "How old are you, son?"

47

"Twelve," he said, removing the hat and running his hand over the fur.

"So you have a bar mitzvah coming up?"

"Yes."

"Well, well, a most auspicious time of your life. Have you been studying?"

"Yes, more or less."

"What does that mean?"

Adam looked embarrassed. "I can't really read the Hebrew, so I'm memorizing it."

"The Hebrew is confusing?"

"I have a learning disorder."

"What sort of disorder?"

"I just have trouble reading and writing."

"But that won't impede your bar mitzvah."

"Of course not," said Dad.

"Well, let's see . . . Moses had his problems too," said Mr. Levin.

"Moses?" I asked.

"Yes. He said, 'I am slow of speech,' so we think perhaps he stuttered or was just extremely shy. It pained him that he couldn't speak easily to his people. But it probably came from the hot coal, do you remember?"

"I think so," I said. We had studied that in school.

"Tell me, young lady."

"Well, when he was a baby, he kept putting on Pharaoh's crown, and there was fear that he might be the one to overthrow Pharaoh. But someone said . . ."

"Jethro," said Mr. Levin.

"Right! Jethro! He said, 'He's just a baby. Test him and you will see.' So they put a hot coal and a . . ."

"A gold piece," said Mr. Levin.

"Yes, a gold piece in front of him. And the Angel Gabriel came down and shoved the coal so that it was very close to Moses, who put it into his mouth."

"What did that mean?" asked Adam.

"That Moses didn't want to be king . . . or Pharaoh . . . right, Mr. Levin?" I asked.

"Yes, very good! He rejected the gold. You are very bright!"

"Thank you." Mom and Dad looked pleased.

"But Moses could also turn a stick into a serpent and back again," said Mr. Levin. "So God gave his brother Aaron the power to do that and to speak for Moses, too."

"Why?" asked Adam.

"So that Moses would have help leading his people to the Promised Land. We all have our battles to fight. God will provide love and help on the day of your bar mitzvah, yes?"

"How about the Angel Gabriel too?" asked Adam.

Mr. Levin smiled. "We could pray for that. And God will understand whatever compromises you have to make."

Dad and Mom were listening. Adam was staring up at this black-bearded man. And between them there was a connection—as if they were meant to meet in a cluttered loft filled with yellow, hazy light.

"I have a little sweet wine and some cake in my office," said Mr. Levin. "Let's celebrate Adam's bar mitzvah."

In his amazingly crowded and dusty office, we sat on rickety folding chairs. Mr. Levin said the prayer over the wine, and we all drank to Adam. Needless to say, I was jealous. But my bas mitzvah had been years before—maybe that's why no one mentioned it.

Mr. Levin made a toast to Dad and Mom. They were very proud, but Adam's face was transformed. He was happier than he had been for a long time.

Mom designed a bed with Mr. Levin, and he gave her a terrific price. It's in my parents' room now, and it's gorgeous. The frame is brass, but the rods are iron, and there are round, fat finials on the posts. And in the curved center of the headboard is a brass angel, which looks a little bit like Adam.

14

Adam
_____

MR. SIMPSON, the science teacher at West Side Prep, waved my notebook paper back and forth.

When I get nervous, I can't hear. I see lips moving, but no sound comes through, like those old movies, where people run around and crash into walls.

"Excuse me, sir?"

"Something wrong with your hearing? I said _'How much time did you spend on this assignment?'_ "

"Most of the evening, sir."

"It's incomplete, and the writing goes all over the page. Don't you type?"

"Sometimes, but with the graphs, it was easier in longhand."

"A mistake, my dear boy. You'll stay after school and repeat the experiment."

"Excuse me, sir?"

"What's the matter with you, Adam? I said, 'You will complete this assignment today!'"

"Excuse me, Mr. Simpson, but I have an appointment today." I had a tutor after school, but I didn't want the other kids to know.

"Cancel it."

Two of my buddies, Dan and Jonathan, turned to look at me. They rolled their eyes and pretended to drool, and some of the other kids giggled.

"Is this funny?" shouted Mr. Simpson.

The lesson had been too hard. I couldn't follow the words down the page and hang onto the logic at the same time. I could memorize for ten minutes, and five minutes later it flew out of my head. And when I had tried to write it down, my pulse thumped so loudly that I couldn't hear my own thoughts.

"Could I come tomorrow instead? I can explain later."

"You'll be here at three o'clock, and you'll stay until this lesson is done . . . if it takes until midnight."

I stood up. "I want to see the headmaster."

"What?" Mr. Simpson stopped waving the paper and took a few steps backward.

"I want to see Mr. French. I'll get him to talk to you."

"Don't be ridiculous. Sit down and be quiet."

"I'll tell him what a jerk you are."

"You'll what?" His mouth fell open.

"You heard me."

"Apologize immediately."

"I won't. You've insulted me. Why can't I insult you?"

"You are not going to the headmaster."

"I am!"

Some of the kids whirled around. Who wants to go to the headmaster? I felt as if I were drowning. I had to leave this room. I had to breathe.

I stumbled up the aisle. The old wooden floor creaked as I bumped against the bolted-down desks. Friendly hands touched me as I moved toward the door.

"One more time, Mr. Brody . . ."

I ran down the marble steps. A truck rumbling toward the park shook the building. Tacked-up messages and notices moved in the air as I passed the bulletin board. It's strange that I noticed all those things because I felt as if I had a temperature of 107 degrees and was about to ignite the whole school.

"I hate him, I'm no good, I'm stupid." It rang through my head. "I hate him, I'm no good, I'm stupid . . ."

Through the glass partition I saw the silhouette of Mr. French at his desk. I knocked. "Come in," he said.

I opened the door and burst into tears.

15

Adam

A CALL to my mother from West Side Prep. Would Mr. and Mrs. Brody and Adam come for a conference? Again.

"His homework is always late," said Mr. Soglio, the dean of boys. "And he doesn't seem to care."

"I do so care!" I said.

Dad put his arm around me. "The work is hard for him."

"Adam, I'm sorry to say this, but you're lazy . . ."

"I'm not lazy!"

". . . you spend a great deal of time socializing."

"Thank God for that," Mom said. "At least he has friends."

Dad sighed. "He's tutored three or four times a week."

"A waste of your money. He needs discipline."

Dad stood up and glowered at Mr. Soglio. "We told you . . . over and over . . . that he's learning-disabled. We begged the school not to take him if you couldn't help him . . ."

"Mr. Brody, he is not learning-disabled. . . ."

"He is!" Mom said. "You pursued him, and you don't even have a remedial teacher."

"Everyone, stop!" I yelled. "Why don't you ask me how *I* feel?"

They all stared at me. The room got very quiet.

"I think I'd like one more chance. I'm not lazy, Mr. Soglio, and I want to learn, but the teachers make me feel hopeless."

"I see. But you've got to buckle down. Do you think you can do that?"

"I'll try!"

"Good. I'll ask the teachers to be more understanding, but this is the last warning you get. Is that clear?"

"Thanks," I said. But I looked at all their faces, and I already knew it was never going to work.

That night I went into my parents' bedroom to say good night. The covers on the bed were turned back, and the lamps were down low. Mom was watching the news, but I could see she wasn't really paying attention.

Dad was straightening his closet. He was doing

it too thoroughly, as if he didn't want to think about anything else.

"Good night, you guys," I said.

Mom said, "This was a difficult day, wasn't it, Adam?"

"The worst," I said. "What if I never get to be normal?"

"Don't say that!" Dad came whizzing out of the closet. "You're going to be fine!"

"We'll work all this out!" Mom said. "Besides, no one is 'normal.' There's no such thing!"

Nightline started. No one switched it off. I wanted to cross the room and huddle against Dad.

Mom smoothed back my hair. "We need to find a new school for you, Adam . . . just in case. West Side Prep is hurting your confidence," she said.

"But I'll have to go through all those tests again, Mom. I can't do it!"

"Darling, somewhere there's a place that will help you. We have to find it."

"I'll make it at West Side. You'll see," I said.

I kissed them and left the room. I figured they had had enough of me for one day. Maybe tomorrow I could make a brand-new start.

16

Caroline

In the summer on Fire Island, our house had a big white-brick fireplace. The family ate dinner in front of it, roasted marshmallows and drowsed off in the late evening when the embers were tiny spots of light. We had friends over to play charades and Scrabble. It was almost as if we had no problems.

But back in New York, when school started again, we all went our separate ways. Too much silence in our apartment. Too many unsaid things. And a lot of yelling too. Not that an actual fireplace would have made a real difference—I know that. It was just, well . . . everything felt too cold, too scheduled, too grim.

Adam was miserable at West Side. It was too

hard for him. He had lots of friends, but he just couldn't cut it. His grades kept going down.

So Mom and Dad were setting up interviews for other schools. There were miles of paperwork spread across the dining room table each night. Endless phone calls, appointments with tutors and teachers.

Meanwhile, I was having trouble too. One of my best friends, Mary Samuels, had been getting stranger and stranger. She lived across the street, and usually we saw each other in the afternoons, even though she went to the Darby School across town.

But lately she wasn't calling me. I was always phoning her and asking her to come over.

"No, thanks, Caroline, I have a big test tomorrow." Or, "Well, my mom wants to buy me new shoes today."

Ordinarily she would have said, "Come along with us," but she didn't. And I knew something was wrong.

One day another friend, Sally Sherman, and I were having a Coke after school, and I said, "Do you have any idea why Mary doesn't seem to like me anymore?"

Sally looked uncomfortable. "I don't know . . ."

"Yes, you do. I can tell you do. Tell me, please, Sally."

"Well, I was at a slumber party the other night . . ."

A slumber party I wasn't invited to. But I just said, "Yes?"

"And she said . . . oh, Caroline, I don't . . ."

"Tell me, please!"

"She said she didn't want to be with you so much."

I could feel my heart pump too hard. It took up so much room that I couldn't breathe. The inside of my mouth got all dry, and I wanted to cry. But not here in the coffee shop.

"Did she say why?"

"Oh, Caroline, I'm sure it was just the way she felt that day. Please don't be upset. Why don't you ask her? I'm so sorry I told you."

"Okay, I'll phone her when I get home."

But I didn't. I went into my room and closed the door. My legs gave out from under me, and I slid down against the wall. And cried and cried. It was as if I heard someone sobbing from far away, but it was me.

The baseboard pressed against my spine. It hurt, but I didn't move. What had I done? Why didn't Mary like me? Why did everything seem spoiled?

Mom knocked at the door. "Darling, what is it?"

I couldn't talk. Mom gave me tissues. Finally I said, "I just heard that Mary doesn't want to be my friend."

"Why?" Mom sat down on the floor and took me in her arms.

"I don't know. I don't know. I feel so bad."

"I know you do, sweetheart, but it couldn't be true. Talk to her."

"I can't, Mom, I can't. It's too humiliating."

"I know, but the only way to solve it is to discuss it."

"Mom, would you call her?"

"Honey, I shouldn't interfere."

"Please!"

So Mom phoned Joanna, Mary's mother, and they had a long talk. I stayed in my room because I didn't want to hear anything. Besides, I couldn't stop crying.

"Caroline, Mary got on the phone too. She says it's just not true."

The next day I was invited to the Samuels' for dinner. Mary and I hugged each other.

"I didn't say those things, Caroline. How could you have believed that?"

"Why would Sally have told me?"

"I don't know. I did say . . ."

"What?"

". . . that it was difficult for us going to different schools. That I didn't think you understood how much work they were giving us."

"No, she didn't say that."

"You should never listen to people who gossip."

"But, Mary, you have been acting weird lately."

"I know. I didn't know how to tell you how

hard everything is now. I stay up so late doing homework that I feel sick all day. I can't eat. I want to leave Darby. There's just too much pressure, but Mom and Dad want me to think it over. I'm really going batty."

"Well, I'm glad you told me."

"And there's one other thing, Caroline . . ."

"What?"

"You seem so upset all the time, but you don't tell anyone what's bothering you."

"Oh. I didn't know it showed. It's Adam, I guess. Everyone is always fussing over him . . ."

"Because he's having such trouble in school?"

"Yes. I wonder if anyone is ever going to notice *me*, although my mom actually did yesterday."

"When she called my mom?"

"It's all so complicated, Mary. Moms calling moms, and daughters crying."

"Like a soap opera," she said, and we hugged each other again.

So we made up. And we are still friends. But I always remember those two days: I honestly thought I would die of grief. And why had Sally told me those things? And what if some of it was true?

I wanted to go to the Darby School with Mary and my other friends, but would they accept me?

I wanted to talk to my parents about it, but they were so worried about Adam that I didn't want to make things worse. Mom had been wonderful, calling Joanna and all, but how could I ask her to do more?

So I kept my dreams a secret. At least for a while.

17

Adam

THE doctor had a brown ponytail, tied with a plaid
Christmas ribbon. Her name was Debbie Leigh, and
she was the best-looking girl I'd ever seen.

She wanted me to tell her my most secret feelings. What I wanted to say was, "Can I take you to
a movie some night?"

But for five days I sat in different rooms in the
Adolescent Division of the hospital and talked to
her and took all the tests: multiple choice, kid-stuff
blocks, inkblot interpretation. And X rays and coordination exercises—everything to show "Who I
was," Debbie said, so they could evaluate me and
help me find the right school.

St. Anne's Hospital was huge and dingy and
beige. Everything was beige. If you were crazy

when you arrived, you'd be crazy and *color-blind* when you left!

But I trusted Debbie, even though it was like confessing to another kid. You know, all the things you'd never tell anyone else.

"Sometimes I'm afraid to go out of the house."

"Why, Adam?"

"Because people will laugh at me or call me 'Dummy.' "

"Has that ever happened?"

"Teachers. They'll see I can't do a paper, and they'll say—in front of the whole class—'Oh, never mind, Adam, I'll just give you something easier.' "

"How does that make you feel?"

"Like dying."

"I'm sure. But you know, you're very smart."

"Maybe. But I feel rotten most of the time."

Dr. Martin, the head of this Adolescent Division, had ordered the tests, but he never showed up while I was at St. Anne's.

"When do I meet him?"

"Later. We do the testing, and he reviews the results. Then we try to find methods to make learning easier for you. And we hope to find the perfect school. This could be the best five days you've ever spent, Adam."

I believed her.

18

Adam

WE were on our way to Dr. Martin's in New Jersey. Across the George Washington Bridge, toward the rough cliffs of the Palisades. It was so clear, we could see way up the river to the little villages in Westchester County.

Mom rolled down the window. Her hand caught the wind. "I wonder what's going to happen."

"What do you mean?" I asked.

Mom turned around. "At our first meeting with him . . ."

"The one where I wasn't invited?" I asked.

"Yes," she said. "I told you—he always wants to interview the parents first. But we were there for an hour, and he wouldn't give us the results of the tests."

"But I've never even seen him!" I said. "How can he know what the tests mean if he's never met me?"

"It's very odd," said Dad, "but everyone says he's a miracle-worker."

Dr. Martin's house in New Jersey looked like something from a grade-B movie.

Pieces of colored glass made a weird design in the stucco. There were dwarflike trees in the front yard, and plastic gnomes and pelicans in the dried-out flower beds. The waiting room smelled sour, and the pictures were all crooked.

Dr. Martin kept trying to pull his jacket down over his belly. And he kept squinting at my mother. I could see she didn't like it. From the beginning, he treated me like a hopeless case.

"Well, Adam, I've gone over your tests . . ."

"What were the results?" Dad asked.

"I'll tell you in good time, Mr. Brody . . ."

"But we expected a report," said Mom.

"Please let me handle this, Mrs. Brody." Mom's eyes got wide, and she sat back in her chair. "And you know, Adam, I've had a meeting with your parents."

"Yes, sir. I'd like to hear the facts." I wanted to say, "and stop squinting at my mother!" but I didn't have the nerve.

"You don't need 'the facts' just yet. I hear you're having trouble at school."

66

"Yes, I guess so. That's why we're here."

" 'Guess?' Don't you know you're making things difficult for yourself?"

Wait a minute. How about, "Can I help you?" Or, "Would you like to talk?" I thought he would be like our pediatrician, Dr. Stone. He might not give me a lollipop, but he didn't have to act like an executioner.

Dad kept staring at his shoes. Mom was fidgeting in her handbag. Suddenly they didn't seem to know me.

Dr. Martin pounded the desk, and we all jumped. He paused for a moment. "Adam, you have caused your parents a lot of grief."

My father held up his hand. "Just a moment, Dr. Martin. We never said . . ."

"Let's not have a battle of wills, Mr. Brody. Adam, are you on drugs?"

"No," I said. "I'm not."

I really wasn't. Not then.

"My assistants tell me you are impaired most of the time."

Mom looked at me. "Adam, are you smoking pot?"

"No!"

"You're lying," Dr. Martin said. He reached over his desk and moved a glass paperweight one inch to the left.

"I'm not doing anything wrong!" Big tears splashed. What a drag. I would have been glad to talk. I would have been *relieved* to tell how bad I felt about the reading and how much I hated my life. Except no one asked.

Dad was on his feet and yelling, "Dr. Martin, my son is not taking drugs. We didn't come here for accusations. We came to get help for his learning problems!"

"Adam, is there something you want to say to your parents?" asked Dr. Dork, ignoring Dad's outburst.

I stood up. "Listen, I don't know where you got your medical license, or who you've ever cured, but I think you're a fake doctor, and they should put you away somewhere."

"Adam!" Mom yanked at my jacket.

"Get me out of here, Dad. Get me out of here!"

"Fine. I can see you enjoy wasting your parents' money and their time." His face was gray and shiny, and his mouth was set in a hard line. He tilted back in his chair and folded his hands over his fat belly.

"Dr. Martin, I think we'll stop," said Dad. "This doesn't seem to be getting us anywhere."

"Not wise, Mr. Brody. You are giving in to your son's problems. These children can be very manipulative."

"Perhaps. But Adam is not 'these children.' He's our son. This isn't what we expect from someone who is supposed to be an expert."

"It's precisely because you came to an expert that you are finally getting the truth. Perhaps you aren't capable of facing the truth."

"We'll call you later," said Mom, gathering up all our coats.

Was she kidding? Over my absolutely dead body. I knew I'd never see this man again. He'd fooled my parents. And I'd always thought they were so smart.

In the car I said, "Why did you let him attack me? He's just a bad, bad guy. He never met me until today. He has no idea who I am. And he doesn't care!" There was a long silence.

"He also needs to wash his clothes," said Mom.

"Ann," said Dad.

"Oh, come on, Jacob, he treated us all like criminals. And he had on one black sock and one brown one."

"He has another pair just like it in his drawer," said Dad. We all started to giggle.

I said, "He squints all the time! *He* should see a doctor."

"We are very disrespectful," said Dad. Suddenly we were all laughing.

Mom clutched her sides and bent forward. "He's a major horror!"

"Right out of a Disney movie," I said.

"He could play the wicked stepmother," said Dad.

"Poor Cinderella would still be sweeping the fireplace," I said.

We were howling by then—not that anything was really that hilarious—but we couldn't stop. And we laughed all the way home.

19

Caroline

ADAM was really upset after the visit to Dr. Martin. He was throwing things in his room . . . yelling at Mom and Dad. That doctor must be a gargoyle. That's the way Adam described him.

I felt sorry for Adam. I mean he was worried about his bar mitzvah, and he had to be interviewed at all these schools. He didn't want to leave West Side; but if he stayed, the monstrous work would just ruin him. It's hard enough if you *don't* have a learning disability.

I tried to comfort him, but there were still so many bad feelings between us, I kind of mumbled and stuttered. But I think he knew what I was trying to say.

I was waiting to hear if I'd be accepted at Darby,

but I didn't have much hope. That's a hard thing to confess, but as Josephine said, "Darlin', may this be the worst thing that ever happens to you." At that time it *was* the worst thing that had ever happened to me.

Daddy was trying to keep on a strong face, but we were just gloom and doom around here. Is that what happens to families who have problems? Sometimes I wished that I were part of another family—the kind with a dog named Spot and a white picket fence in the country.

What a joke! The Brodys are all glued to the streets of New York. The sidewalks, the stores, the theaters, the cafes, our friends, the skyscrapers, Riverside Park, and the museums. I couldn't imagine living in another city, but maybe somewhere else it wouldn't be so . . . what's the word I want? Emotional! It wouldn't be so emotional! And all this pretending that everything would be all right.

What if everything would never be all right? I couldn't stand even thinking about that.

20

Adam

I DIDN'T know there were so many private schools in New York City. And I was dragged to practically every one of them. Or at least to the ones that said they had a program for dyslexic kids.

There's this process, you see, where you first apply to a school. You take another ERB test. You send all your class records, and then you go for an interview and a tour. And each school has its own test, so you sit in an empty room and write or draw or do whatever they want.

Then you wait for weeks to hear whether or not you got in.

One of the schools had a new gym, and the interviewer, who was in an orange dashiki, said, "Adam, glad you're interested in athletics. That's a strong part of our program here at the Mark School."

Fantastic, I thought. I'll get to be on a team.

Then there was a school with no walls. No kidding . . . just partitions. You could hear every class and every teacher from wherever you sat. It was like a madhouse. I knew I could never learn there, but the admissions director said, "We take students like Adam very often."

"How would I concentrate with all that noise?" I asked.

"You'll learn to focus quickly and more fully," she said. "We also have remedial classes after school. And all the teachers are called by their first names."

I almost laughed. Would that make a difference? If I called a teacher by the last or the first name, would I learn to read better? I couldn't believe she held that out as a reason to go to the Carson School.

Nevertheless, it sounded pretty good. I knew a lot of the kids there, and it was just two blocks from our apartment. And they really seemed to want me to enroll, so maybe I could get used to the no walls and do well. Wasn't it worth a try?

Anyway, it was nice just to be fussed over. At the Wilton School, on the East Side, the principal said, "Yes, we know Adam didn't do brilliantly on the ERB test, but he was just terrific in the interview. And our music program would benefit him."

Mom and Dad began to relax a little as the

weeks went by. It looked as if I would actually have a choice! Who would have thought?

I began to have dreams about a new school where I wouldn't be the dumbest one—where I could make a fresh start.

"Adam, we're so proud of you," Dad said. We had just left a school called New York Day and Country, where they spent a lot of time outdoors studying the city and the farmlands in New Jersey and Connecticut. It sounded incredible.

"Mrs. Brown, the interviewer, said you were one of the most interesting boys she had seen," Mom said. "She's practically assured you a place." She was smiling down at me. (I was still disgustingly short.)

"Yeah, that school seems terrific."

"Well, chances are you can go there if you want," Dad said. "People are recognizing all the good things about you, as well they should."

"Absolutely," Mom said.

We visited gyms, classrooms, cafeterias, swimming pools, science labs, libraries. We talked to a million people. I smiled and tried to be perfect until I was turning blue. But finally we finished around the end of March.

The first letter came in early April.

"Did the Wilton School say 'yes,' Mom?"

"Well, they . . . feel it's not quite right for you."

"But they were wild about Adam," Dad said.

Mom looked puzzled. "Don't worry, honey, you'll be accepted at lots of other schools."

Then the New York Day and Country wrote, "We feel Adam should probably be in a more traditional atmosphere." What? They practically hugged me when I left that day. They would have taken Dad's tuition check in a minute! What had happened?

A letter from the guy in the dashiki: "Thank you for applying, but Adam's interests will probably not be met by our programs."

"I must have bombed out on the test."

"You did just fine," said Dad, tearing up the letter.

"Then why are you so mad?" I asked.

"Because it doesn't make any sense. They even said that they would pay special attention to you if we'd let you attend."

"And we know you'd be an asset to them," said Mom.

All the letters were like that. Twelve of them!

Mom and Dad were grim all the time, while pretending not to be. Caroline was actually sympathetic. "It'll be okay, Adam," she said, "you'll find a school." And Jo kept bringing me plates of food. "I made fried chicken for you, hon."

But nothing helped. All the schools had rejected me. Why had they changed their minds? I felt so rotten that I could hardly talk to anyone. My work at West Side just stopped. I couldn't concentrate on anything.

The future didn't just look discouraging—it had *vanished*.

21

Caroline

Mom does one thing when she's upset. She howls. Like a coyote in acute distress.

About four in the morning I heard the howling. You could have heard it on Broadway and Forty-second Street.

I walked through the long hall, the foyer, the butler's pantry, the living room. Mom was rocking back and forth on the sofa.

Daddy was kneeling down, his hand on her head. "Ann, Dr. Martin should be put in jail, but . . ."

"I feel so sad. I feel so sad. I feel so sad." Her face was swollen and red from crying. How long had she been here? The front of her nightgown was drenched.

"I know, darling, but come on, let's talk."

"Jacob, I can't."

"Yes, you can! You're overreacting to the point of craziness. Now stop it!"

"I can't. What are we going to do?"

"We'll find an answer. Now lift your head and let me dry your eyes."

"Oh God, oh God, oh God . . ."

Then they saw me.

"Caroline, what are you doing up?" Daddy was flustered. I knew they didn't want me here, but I had already heard a lot, so I wasn't going to leave.

"What's happening?"

"You're happier not knowing." It was one of Daddy's standard jokes, but this time it didn't sound so funny.

"Come on! You woke me up! Tell me what's going on!"

"Tell her, Jay."

Daddy gave Mom an angry look. "All right! But I think it's a mistake . . ."

"Tell her, Jay!" Her rocking back and forth grew worse, and her sobs were like the hiccoughs of a little kid who was cried out.

"Look, Caroline, that Dr. Martin we took Adam to see . . . ?"

"That awful guy in New Jersey?"

"Yes," said Mom, "that monster."

"He sent the hospital reports to all the schools that we're applying to for Adam."

"What does that mean?"

"It means," said Dad, "that every admissions department in the city knows the results of his psychological tests—his problems, his fears, his feelings of failure."

"And his dreams," said Mom. "Even his dreams!"

"Instead of . . . ?" I asked.

"Instead of a simple report that says, 'this kid is dyslexic, but he's able to learn,' " said Dad. "That's the kind of report he was supposed to send—not the results of the psychological tests. Those are supposed to be strictly confidential."

"God! Dr. Martin did that? Why?"

"We don't know," Mom said. "Maybe because we stormed out of his office and never went back."

"How did you find out?"

"A woman called us from the Carson School," said Mom. "She said that they had just loved Adam —and were going to accept him—but then they got this report, and the admissions people were afraid he would be disruptive."

"She said that she could lose her job for telling us, but she was so shocked by what Dr. Martin did, she had to call," said Dad, looking weary. "No one else had the guts to do it."

"Poor Adam," I said. I felt sick. This was really the pits.

"I don't know what we're going to do," said Mom.

"There will be a school for Adam," said Dad. "Now dry your eyes."

"Oh God, oh God, oh God . . ."

"Ann, I have twenty people depending on me tomorrow. It's the first rehearsal for the new show. I must go to bed." Dad's voice was wavery.

"I don't care about your show. I don't care."

"Well, you'd better care!"

You could also hear Dad on Broadway and Forty-second Street. You could open two shows: "Ann Howls," and "Jacob Howls Too." Have your tickets ready, folks.

I had never heard my parents argue like this before. They must have kept me in a bubble-world. I didn't want to hear anymore.

I started toward the door. "Honey, we're sorry you woke up. I know this is shocking news," said Mom, "but please don't ever, ever tell Adam."

"Mother, do you think I'm that mean?"

"Of course not, but this is a big secret to carry around."

As I walked toward my room, I could hear their voices rising again.

"Jay, that boy doesn't have a school for next year. There's no place in the world for him! And it's all my fault."

"It's not your fault."

"Yes, it is. I gave him all these bad genes."

I got into bed. What had become of our family? We used to laugh and goof around and have fun. Things might get worse, but as I turned out the light, it didn't seem remotely possible.

22

Adam

FINALLY I transferred to the Amy Evans School in Greenwich Village. I left early and went down into the dark subway. All my friends were walking to West Side Prep, and I felt as if I were being sent to prison.

In New York everyone reads on the train . . . everyone! Books, magazines, newspapers, letters, homework, office memos. Some people know how to arrange *The New York Times* so that it's in four long sections. They fold over one section at a time. How can they read so calmly while the train is swaying, and noisy crowds are rushing in and out?

You see the tops of all these reading heads—red hair, blond hair, no hair, baseball caps, yarmulkes, babushkas, ponytails, braids, Afros. I wanted to read too. At least I wanted to pretend to read so that I didn't look like such an idiot.

So I learned to sound out the words of the signs, the ones that advertise hemorrhoid cures and beauty schools and dental plans. I walked up and down and read them over and over again. My lips were moving, but I was really reading. And if a friend from Amy Evans got on the car, he would see me walking up and down and moving my lips and he would know that I was not so dumb as I seemed in class.

And there were the poetry cards. Each month some New Yorker's poem would be printed along with a little drawing and some information about the writers. Office workers or students or housewives. They wrote about sunsets or love or loneliness. Stuff like that.

Sometimes they made me cry, which was not terrific, as I didn't want anyone to think I was having a mini-breakdown right there on the Broadway Local No. 1, which actually, I probably was.

23

Adam

It was our last Fire Island tennis game for the season. Almost all the houses had been closed, and leaves crinkled under our feet.

A sea gull flew so low that it looked like the ball I was trying to smash back to Dad.

I crouched down, and the wings flapped past my head.

"Adam, take that over. I think they've got a little clubhouse in the tree behind you."

"Thanks, I will." We finished the point, and I won the set. We shook hands, and Dad kissed me. He always does that, and although it's pretty embarrassing, I do kind of like it.

"You're really good, Adam." We were drinking

iced tea afterward on the benches in front of the funky general store. "Your coordination is beautiful. Now you have to get more instruction and play as much as you can."

"Wish we had tennis at Amy Evans," I said.

"There's a boarding school in New Jersey, the Eckhardt School, that has one of the best teams in the East."

"Yeah, but I don't go there."

"But you could."

"No, I couldn't. And I never will. I'm not going away! Chill out, Dad."

"Adam . . ."

"Sorry." I took off my shoes. "So what's for dinner?"

"Bluefish, I think." A long silence. "One of Mommy's friends has a son who went there and loved it."

"I'm not going to some nerd school in New Jersey."

"It's not a 'special' school. They only take a few dyslexic kids. And you go to the same classes as everyone else. But you have your own tutor every day."

"Why can't I just go to public school in New York?"

"Because there's not one that has a real remedial program. We've looked into all of them."

"But it's so expensive! And I'd be lonely away from home."

"You might be for a while, but then you might love accomplishing things! Why don't you have your bar mitzvah and then reconsider?"

"Dad! I miss my friends from West Side as it is. If I go that far away, I'll never get to see them, even on weekends. And you know . . . when I think of my bar mitzvah, I get spaced-out."

"Listen for one minute . . ."

"Dad, in thirty words or less, please."

"You are going to have a wonderful, meaningful ceremony."

"Okay, I'm going to be an ideal Jew every day for the rest of my life. No bacon . . ."

"Adam!"

"Give me a yarmulke, please . . ."

"Adam!" Dad put his arm around my throat in a mock stranglehold.

"I want to be perfect!"

"You don't have to be perfect, you fresh kid. All you have to do is enjoy the moment. It's your moment—no one else's."

We turned the bikes up our street. Two mangy deer, totally unafraid, crossed in front of us. We braked to keep from hitting them.

"They don't have to study for a bar mitzvah," I said.

"They don't get to play tennis either."

We laughed. I looked across the bay as a fishing boat sailed by.

"Okay," I said. "I'm going to do both."

"That's my boy."

"But I'm still scared about the bar mitzvah."

"I understand."

"And I still miss my friends."

"I believe that's called 'having the last word.' "

"You bet, Pop."

We rode the rest of the way home.

24

Adam

I STUDIED for a year with Rabbi Hirsch and Cantor Berman, the "singer" for the congregation. Sometimes we'd have such a good time singing that we'd end up hugging each other. "Adam," he'd say, "only angels have voices like yours."

I practiced and practiced until I knew my bar mitzvah service by heart.

"If you want, I'll help you memorize," Caroline said. "Mom drilled me for weeks, remember?"

I was surprised. She actually seemed interested, not angry. "Thanks, I'm totally crazed."

"Don't be. Just look at the audience. Uncle Paul always pushes out his false teeth at the most emotional moments. He did it at my ceremony when we all marched around the temple with the Torah."

The "portion" of the Torah that I was to read was about Abraham sacrificing Isaac on the mountain. How could Abraham consider that, even if God was speaking through the clouds in that big booming voice?

"Rabbi Hirsch, why didn't Isaac say, 'Dad, let's not rush into anything'?"

The rabbi laughed. "Scholars have debated that for centuries, Adam. Abraham must have had a strong, mysterious faith."

"Would you put your son on an altar like that?"

He paused for a long time. "Well, I think I would have been very troubled. But I admire your inquisitive mind."

I loved these discussions! My brain was waking up!

On the Big Morning I was in a numb haze. I had a new suit, and Dad came in to help me with my tie. His hands shook a little. He kissed me and said, "Break a leg, Adam." I loved his saying it because it's a theatrical expression which means, "Good luck."

The sun was spilling through the stained glass windows, and the temple was really full: classmates, relatives from all over the country, my parents' best friends, teachers from the synagogue school and from Amy Evans, Fire Island neighbors, and the doctor who delivered me!

As the service began, Dad and I stood up and sang a duet. I saw handkerchiefs come out and there was a lot of sniffing. And yes! there was

Uncle Paul, big tears rolling down his face, his false teeth sticking out in the air. It was hilarious, and I did laugh! Caroline had been right: suddenly I relaxed.

Then Rabbi Hirsch handed the Torah to Dad, who started shaking so much that the silver ornaments danced. He has a tremor when he gets emotional. We looked at each other. When I smiled, he calmed down and held my hand for a minute.

The cantor stayed by my side as I read my "portion." Everyone was absolutely silent. And smiling. My memorized Hebrew seemed to be working.

The rabbi put his hands on my head and spoke so that only I could hear. "I'm so proud of you, Adam. You are very gifted, and you're going to have a happy, fulfilled life." I don't know why, but I started to cry, and I couldn't stop.

So my bar mitzvah was finally over. I had read a story I didn't like and didn't understand. How could a father give up his son like that? And now that I was finished, I felt guilty about getting millions of presents. I felt bad that the party would cost Dad and Mom so much money. And I was sure I had "faked" the reading.

But I had survived the test. Even now, years later, I'm not sure what happened. I really did work hard, but would Rabbi Hirsch say it had been "faith"? Mr. Levin, the Orthodox Jew at the brass-bed workshop, had said "God understands compromises." Did I believe there was a God looking down on me that day? Was I a good Jew, even though I couldn't read Hebrew? I don't know. I've never stopped wondering about it, and I guess I never will.

25

Caroline

ADAM was always with a gang of boys. At home they went into his room and cranked up the stereo.

The rock music was eardrum-bursting. I'd ask Adam to turn it down, so that I could get my homework done. And he would do it. For about ten minutes.

Then he and his friends would start to laugh and yell. They would get out on the fire escape and smoke marijuana, and the smell would come right through my window, and the music would be turned up again.

Wasn't this my home too? Why did I have to ask for quiet? Why didn't Josephine say something to them? I knew she could smell that dope. Why weren't Mom and Dad ever home in the afternoon? We were all victims of Adam's life.

Even the elevator men had their opinions. Hector said, "You should tell your parents, Caroline, those boys are a bad influence on Adam."

"How can I do that, Hector? Mom and Dad will just accuse me of being mean or of being a tattle-tale."

"You're right. Those kids are rude to me too. Always hanging on the buzzer. They never say 'thank you.' Well, Adam does. But his friends shouldn't be allowed to come here anymore. Particularly Timothy Kim."

"He stayed with us last night. His father threw him out again."

"I know. They had a big fight in the lobby."

This was bad enough. But I had finally heard from the Darby School. They had only one open place, and it was not going to be mine. Mom was sympathetic, but Dad said, "Well, on to the next . . ." And I tried to forget about it.

One day The Grateful Dead was so loud that my room was shaking. I got furious and called Adam, "fat." It just came out of my mouth.

Josephine came to my door. "Caroline, I want to talk to you."

"I hate him, Jo!"

"That's clear, honey. May I come in?"

"If you want."

She sat down. "Why do you call him 'fat'? Don't you know he's having enough to deal with as it is?"

"He's funny looking, and that music is killing me!"

"What's bothering you these days? You know he's not 'funny looking.' You're like a cat on fire."

"If I tell you, don't laugh."

"I'd never laugh at you."

"Well . . . oh . . ."

"Tell me, cookie."

"I just feel . . . that I can't tell Mom and Dad anything! So it feels . . . lonely." I stamped my foot. "Oh, Jo, don't tell them I said that."

"I promise. But you've got to be kind to your brother."

"If he would just get those guys out of the house!"

"He will. Even if I have to say something to your folks. But Adam is the closest blood relative you'll ever have . . ."

"Oh, pu-u-ulease, Jo!"

". . . except for your own children . . . and if you don't get to be friends . . ."

"Well, I might try." I wished I wasn't too big to sit on her lap. "But not today."

She stroked my hair, just the way she did when I was little. Then she went back into the kitchen.

I felt a little better. I hated to sound like a whiner, but it was a relief to talk to someone. Especially Jo.

I lay on the bed and stared at the ceiling. Mom and Dad were both beginning new projects. I was glad that they loved their work, but they were always late coming home for dinner, and then they spent the evening on the phone, with scripts and papers all over the place.

The house felt like a boat being tossed around in the water, throwing us all from side to side, with no real captain at the helm.

26

Adam

At the Whitney Museum they had an exhibit of this sculptor, Duane Hanson. He makes life-size statues of people reading letters, listening to the radio, sitting in real chairs. You'd swear they were alive.

Ron and Timothy and I went to see the Hansons. We made up stories about all the figures. For a statue who was leaning over, we said, "He just ate a bad hamburger." Or for a man and woman who looked totally stunned: "Their daughter just flunked out of school." Stuff like that.

We decided to *be* the statues. We sat on the floor, against the walls, and froze. It's amazing how totally still you can become if you just get quiet inside. Pull back your breathing and try not to think about anything that's bothering you. And we weren't even stoned.

Some little kids came by. "Wow! Don't they look *real?*" one of them asked.

It was the happiest I'd been in a long time. I had my friends with me. We were doing this crazy, wonderful thing. And no one was telling me I was lazy, or stupid, or behind in my schoolwork.

Other days we'd go to movies. We'd sit in the balcony and bliss out on joints. The first time I did that, I didn't think anything was happening.

But soon I thought I was seeing words come around a corner. "Just a minute," I said. "The word 'car' is going to come in view. Wait! Here comes 'window' too." I frantically tried to capture the images in my mind, but they kept rounding out of sight. I felt so frustrated.

But from that day on I smoked a lot. I was rolling so many joints with Zigzag brand paper, I really was "Adam Zigzag." That seemed incredibly funny, especially when I was stoned. But the guys never knew why I was laughing. I didn't want them to know anything about my nickname and how I felt about myself.

When the movie was over, we'd wait in the lobby for a half hour and then slip back into another theater and see the second movie.

If my parents weren't home, we'd go back to my house and jam or play tapes. That's what my sister hated: the noise and the beer drinking, with the smell of pot slipping under her door.

27

Adam

"My report card is lousy, right?"

"Not as good as it could be, Adam." Dad looked up from where he sat on the couch. The Mozart Fifteenth Piano Concerto was playing. It's Dad's favorite. Funny how you remember little details.

"Dad, I'm sorry."

"We should talk about this. The reading is getting harder?"

"No! It's just the usual! I hate school."

"All right," he said. "You have to do something."

"Yeah, jump off a cliff, I guess."

"Adam! Are you that desperate? Tell me!" He pulled me down beside him.

"No, no . . . I just said that."

He put his arm around me and held on. After a minute, he said, "Mom and I heard of a doctor, Fred Covan, who is great with teenagers."

"What kind of doctor?"

"A psychologist."

"Where'd you hear about him?"

"A friend of mine. He has a son with a learning problem too."

"Oh, great. Another misfit."

"I want you to call Covan."

"I can't believe you! A shrink! He'll tell me to go to boarding school! That's what you'd like me to do!"

"We don't know what he might say. Isn't it worth a try? But you're so unhappy lately. Once upon a time Mom and I knew how to help you. But these days . . ."

"No! I don't want to leave another school. Can't you understand that? I'd have to make friends all over again."

"You're out of control, Adam. I keep asking if you're smoking pot . . ."

"I'm not!"

"I think you are!"

"Oh, Dad, you are so out of it . . ."

Dad took my shoulders and shook me. "Don't throw your life away. Please, please let us help you." He sat down and started to cry. Uncontrollably. In front of me. I wanted to die. I knew that I was the cause of his grief. But fathers are not supposed to cry.

"Dad, Daddy . . . I'm sorry." I knelt down. "I'll do something. I'll think about going to the doctor. Please don't cry!"

We looked at each other. The Mozart had ended, and the needle was scratching across the record, back and forth and back and forth.

28

Adam

"ONCE there were some people. Alice, Jackie, David, and Adam. They were afraid of baby-sitting. David was scared of baby-sitting (because he had just seen the movie, *When a Stranger Calls*). He took the job because he needed the money.

"When David arrived, he was given instructions on what to do in case there was trouble. David felt very jumpy when all of a sudden the phone rang. It frightened him so much he had a heart attack. (poor dave)

"Needing money for the funeral, Alice and Jackie took a baby-sitting job together. (at the same house) The phone rang. Jackie was so scared, she jumped up and ran into the wall and broke her face. And Alice ran out of the house only to slip on the

wet porch breaking her back and getting a concu-
sion.

"Needing money for three funerals, smart
Adam takes a baby-sitting job at the same house.

"The phone rang. Smart Adam knew what to
do. He picked up the phone and blew a whistle into
the receiver, breaking the caller's ear drum.

"The moral of this story is whistle while you
work."

Mrs. Lubow read my paper carefully. She was
Tutor Number Five. Everyone else had given up.

"Adam, do you know the word 'macabre'?"

"Oh, weird . . . spooky?"

"Exactly. You found a humorous way to handle
a serious subject."

"Thanks."

"We'll talk about paragraphs. 'Concussion' has
two s's. And parentheses depend upon whether
they're a part of the sentence . . ."

"Or whether they stand alone?"

"You're way ahead of me."

"Why can't I get that all straight?"

Mrs. Lubow laughed. "Stop being so hard on
yourself. Now when's the history test?"

"Friday."

"I'll remind your teacher that the test be un-
timed. Then you'll be more relaxed. Let's look at the
math for tomorrow."

I liked Mrs. Lubow. She told me exactly what I
needed to do. Why couldn't my parents be like
that? More strict, I guess. I think they were afraid of

100

me. I hated feeling that I was getting away with murder. But I was, and we all knew it.

I was in a real rut: getting up, getting high, taking more dope at school, cheating on every test, coming home to face homework I couldn't do.

I hid grass everywhere. Some I kept in a huge toy kangaroo in my room—in the pouch with the baby kangaroo peeking over the edge. I unhooked the back of my radio and kept stuff in there. No one noticed that there were no screws in the back panel.

Down deep somewhere I think my parents knew. Dad was asking me about it more and more. But he didn't really want the truth.

There was no order in my life, no demands, no expectations. Sometimes I felt that maybe Mom and Dad didn't have any hope for me either. I felt totally abandoned.

One day I walked out of history class without permission and came back stoned. My teacher, Mr. Darrid, was really upset, and a terrible sorrow washed over his face. He put his hand on my shoulder and said, "Hello! Anyone in there?"

"Yeah, I'm here, sir."

"Adam, can I help you with this chapter? The Boston Tea Party too boring?"

"No, sir. I just can't seem to lock it in."

"Going out into the hall without permission won't solve the problem."

I put my head into my hands. I couldn't cry in front of everyone!

"Come see me after class, Adam. Let's talk. I'll bring Cokes or something."

But I didn't go. I got on the crowded, dirty train at three o'clock. I was failing everything, everyone. Even standing up Mr. Darrid, who was probably waiting for me in Room 103, with the Cokes making wet rings on the desk.

I had to do something about my life. I started thinking. Should I go away? Maybe at that boarding school, I could start over.

29

Adam

THE Addams Family could have lived at the Eckhardt School. Ivy all over the place, and towers with dark, small windows.

Inside a chandelier was being cleaned by a guy on a ladder. Bowls of flowers were on all the tables, and a big room—like a ballroom—looked out on a garden, where kids were playing touch football.

The admissions officer, Mrs. Becker, gave us tea in her office. "We only take twenty-five special students, and they go to the same classes as everyone else."

"But how can they keep up?" I asked.

"Your tutor will prepare you each day for every class . . . until you can be on your own. And you must repeat the ninth grade when you enter Eckhardt next September."

"What?" I nearly yelled.

"Adam, be honest," said Mrs. Becker. "Don't you think it's interesting that you've come this far in school, but you really can't read well?"

"I suppose so."

"Sometimes students are passed to the next level because the teacher knows they're smart, or because it's just too much trouble to really teach them. We don't allow that to happen here."

"What if I can't make it?"

"You can make it. You're very intelligent, but you need to catch up."

"How will I do it?"

"You'll learn ways to improve your skills."

"Tricks?"

"No. We call them 'Learning Skills.' And we have a very high success rate."

Not with me, they wouldn't. But she had my attention.

"Would you like a tour of the school?"

"Wonderful," said Dad.

Mrs. Becker pushed a buzzer, and a tall boy in a blue jacket and striped tie appeared in the doorway. Mr. Preppy.

"This is Benjamin McDonald. He's an official guide for the month."

He shook hands with everyone and pulled out Mom's chair as she rose. Weenie, I thought. Did he actually like dragging people around?

In the dining room everyone seemed to be having a good time. How could they, so far from home?

"Ben, you've had a good experience at Eckhardt?" asked Dad.

"Yes, sir. This place saved my life."

"How?" I asked.

"Well, for the first time, I felt I had a chance . . ."

Mom and Dad exchanged a look. Hm-m-m. Maybe there was hope after all. But if I'd loused up at every other school, with every single tutor, I could do it here. And then I wouldn't have any other place to go. This was the end of the line.

The library looked over the track and football fields to the hills in the distance. Sunshine covered the long tables and chairs and green plants growing in the corners. Not bad.

The swimming pool and the gym were new. The dormitory rooms were crowded with bunk beds, posters, and dirty laundry piled in corners. Notebooks, pencils, pens, T squares were scattered everywhere. Well, real people lived here anyway.

The English class sat in a circle. Only ten kids. At least you'd get some attention, if you had anything to say.

"What do you think, Adam?" asked Dad as we were riding back to New York.

"I hate the ties and jackets."

"But that's not a reason, is it?" Mom turned around in the front seat.

"It's good enough." I leaned over and put on a cassette of The Rowdy Boys.

"Turn that down, please," said Dad.

"Okay. Chill out, Dad."

There was a pause. "I'm not crazy about that expression, Adam."

"Sorry. Anyway, how can we afford that school?"

"We'd find a way." But he looked worried. "Listen, it's a good thing: No rock concerts. Definite study hours, great team sports."

"They probably have terrible food." I lay down on the backseat and began singing to the music.

"Please, not so loud," begged Mom.

"Can't I do anything right?"

The Manhattan skyline popped up, like a kid's cutout book. The top of the Empire State Building glowed yellow. We were silent.

It's too scary, I thought. I'm not going away, I'm not going away, I'm not going away . . .

30

Caroline

"CAROLINE," Miranda said, "want to study for the geometry test?"

"Sure!" Miranda was a genius at math. And besides, I really liked her.

"Can we go to your house?" she asked. "My mom's got the flu."

"Yes . . ." I prayed that gang of thugs wouldn't be in Adam's room.

We had been working about an hour when Adam knocked on the door. I looked at him carefully. He gets "too happy" when he smokes pot, but he looked almost like his old, cute self.

"Miranda! It's great to see you." He gave her a big hug.

"Hey, Adam, how's the new school?"

"Okay. But I miss everybody at West Side."

"We miss you too. The halls are too quiet."

"Well, I'm making up for that at Amy Evans. Josephine asked if you wanted cocoa. Any takers?"

"Me," I said.

Miranda held up her hand. "Me too."

"Me three," said Adam. "I'll bring it to you."

"Want some help?" asked Miranda.

"No, study on. Back soon."

Miranda said, "I thought he was stoned all the time?"

"He usually is. But not today."

"He seems terrific. I get the feeling he doesn't like Amy Evans much."

"Yeah," I said, "it must be a drag." Why hadn't I thought about that?

When Adam came back, we all sat on the floor and drank our chocolate and ate Josephine's shortbread cookies. He played some records—country and folk music, Miranda's favorites. We sang along with James Taylor and the Gatlin Brothers and Emmylou Harris. Adam even brought in his guitar and taught Miranda some chords.

"You're an incredible learner," he said.

"You're an incredible teacher, Adam. How's your band doing?"

"We're composing our own stuff now."

"Could I listen sometime?"

"Sure, if it's okay with Caroline. The guys make a lot of commotion."

Where had this thoughtful person been?

"It's fine with me," I said. "Just give me warning."

"Well, I'd better get out of here." He picked up the tray. "Call me if you need any help. You know how brilliant I am at math."

I felt so sad. He couldn't do math at all. We all knew it, but we just laughed. He closed the door and Miranda said, "He's so nice, Caroline. He's going to be just fine, don't you think?"

"Yes." And I wanted to believe it. Maybe I would get my brother back again.

31

Adam

"Ir you press against the frets like this," Tim said, "it makes a better sound."

"Ouch!"

I put down the guitar and rubbed my fingers. Timothy laughed. "You'll get used to it, Adam. The calluses just move to a different place."

"You're an amazing musician, Tim. Your dad has taught you so much."

"Yeah. When he's not throwing me out of the house."

"My parents said you can always stay here."

"I know. But if they knew that we smoke so much . . . I wish I could stop."

"Me too. Sometimes I hate it."

"Adam . . ."

"What?"

"You're going to find something you're good at too."

"If I could just crack the reading . . ."

"You will."

"We are some pair! Wanna play some more, Tim?"

"Sure. How about some James Taylor?"

We tuned our guitars and leaned against the wall.

"Watch your fingers on the frets, Adam."

I did exactly as he told me. The music sounded better.

32

Caroline

EACH morning was always the same.

"Dad, I can't go to school. I have a temperature."

"Adam, you don't."

"Yes, feel my forehead. I'm really sick."

"You're cool as can be," Mom said.

"I twisted my ankle. See? I'm limping."

After a hurried breakfast, he couldn't find his books.

"I put them here on the desk. They're gone!"

I said, "They're in the living room, under the sofa."

"Now I remember. I was using the encyclopedia."

"And you fell asleep too," I said.

"Caroline!" said Mom.

I was sorry I'd blurted that out. I wasn't trying to be mean, but Mom and Dad were frantic. Couldn't they see that Adam was hung over? And maybe from something worse than pot? LSD or cocaine? Lots of kids were into those too.

"Dad, *I can't go to school!*"

He bumped into the wall.

"Ow!"

I felt bad for Adam, but as he made us all rush around and yell, I'd get furious. I was almost ready to scream at Mom and Dad, "Can't you see he's high all the time? Do something!" But he was my brother, and I couldn't bring myself to rat on him.

Mom started toward her bedroom. Some of the coffee in her cup splashed onto the floor. I got a towel and wiped it up.

"Adam, get your coat *now!*" Dad's face was turning red, and he was shaking more than usual.

"Sorry, Dad, I'm not trying to make you angry."

"It's just that I'm getting a reputation for being late to rehearsal."

"Okay, I'm gone, Dad. You can be too."

Daddy took him to the door and threw a scarf around Adam's neck. I followed them out. Not waiting for the elevator, Adam thumped down the stairs, two at a time. On the first landing he stopped and called, "I love you, Dad."

Daddy's eyes misted. I could almost see his heart turn over.

33

Adam

THE idea of vacation was a joke. Even when school was in session, I was on vacation, stoned most of the time.

For the first part of Christmas break, I went to Los Angeles, where my mom was shooting a picture. Dad stayed home because Caro's vacation didn't come until a week later.

I only stayed a week, but it was unbelievable. Lots of Mexican food, no lessons, no fights with my sister, and no dope. I didn't turn on once.

Mom drove me to the airport. She didn't walk me to the gate because I was too old to have my mother put me on a plane. We said good-bye at the curb. She looked very teary, but I pretended not to notice.

The agent told me the plane was delayed five hours. Five hours! I ran outside, but she was gone. I had enough money, but what would I do for five hours?

I couldn't remember the phone number at the rented house, and it was unlisted.

I couldn't remember the address either. And my mother wouldn't even be there. She was headed for a party in the San Fernando Valley. What was the name of the family she was visiting?

I called New York to get the information from Dad. Only the machine answered.

But I knew where the key to Mom's house was hidden. I'd go back there and at least have a comfortable place to wait. I fantasized that Mom would say, "Oh, just stay on. You missed your plane, so why not forget school too?"

In the men's room I lit a joint, my first since I'd been in Los Angeles. I got a taxi, and the driver said, "What street in Brentwood?"

"It's near a school called Paul Revere."

We circled around the school and went up three or four roads off Mandeville Canyon. I was getting more and more mixed-up, and now it was really dark.

The driver stopped the car. "Listen, you know I should take you to the cops. You're buzzed out of your mind."

"Just take me back to the airport," I said. "I

don't know what you're talking about." He grunted, but he did it.

The cab cost thirty-five dollars. My money was almost gone. I had really botched up everything. Too dumb to remember a phone number. Too afraid of words to write things down.

In a men's room stall, I made another joint. Zig-zag paper, of course. There must have been something bad mixed in it because in about three minutes I was on the floor, the ceiling circling over my head.

The next thing I remember is going down the escalator and being terrified that I'd keel over or get my foot caught at the bottom.

A woman shook her finger at me and shrieked, "I should get the police, you junkie!" I thought, "Doesn't matter, lady. This is my last day on Earth." But my jaw seemed clamped shut. I couldn't open it to ask for help.

I staggered into a cafeteria for coffee, but couldn't make my hands stop shaking to get out the money. As I headed for a bench, a man shouted, "Are you crazy?"

Two hours later I managed to get on the plane. I looked like Swamp Man. By that time I was making swamplike noises, too.

The stewardesses covered me with blankets. I slept until we landed at Kennedy. Dad was there with the car. He kept feeling my forehead and saying, "You have a terrible fever." I just kept changing the subject.

But I knew I had better do something fast. I didn't want to die. I was sick of feeling like some lowlife. And if I could learn to read and write decently, I would never have to be lost again, wandering around in the dark, looking for my mother.

34

Adam

DR. COVAN didn't look like a shrink. His blue jeans had holes in the knees. A denim jacket flapped open over a checked flannel shirt, and there was a motorcycle parked in front of his office, which was in the basement of a brownstone.

"You were brave to call me the other day. That takes guts."

"Yeah . . . but this is probably going to be a big waste of time."

"Maybe, Adam. Maybe not. Don't think 'no.' "

"What goes on in my head is not very interesting."

"Tell me anyway. I got into this business because I'm extremely nosy."

"I don't know why I called."

"Have you ever been in therapy before?"

"Yeah. This guy on Fifth Avenue. All we did was play cards in his crummy office." Dr. Covan smiled at me. "I'm serious! He thought it was so relaxing that I'd spill everything . . ."

"And of course you didn't."

"Right. But I learned to play a mean game of Go-Fish."

"How long did you go?"

"The whole sixth grade. But one day I told my folks I wasn't going to go anymore."

"And . . . they agreed?"

"Yes. They never make me do anything. They shouldn't have given in so quickly."

"Did you tell them that?"

"No, I couldn't." I rubbed the leather arm of the sofa. "They feel bad enough about me. And they're spending all this money."

"Why did your parents want you to see a therapist then?"

"Oh, I was running all over the school, and I couldn't read. I still can't read."

"I see. You're in the ninth grade now?"

"Yep."

"Was there any other therapy?"

"Well, just this other creep, once, in New Jersey. I really hated him!"

"What happened?"

"I walked out and never went back."

"Did you tell *him* how you felt?"

"Yes, right at that moment."

"Okay. We might be able to work together. How would you feel about coming here regularly?"

"How many times will I have to see you?"

"It depends upon what you want."

Well, this doctor rode a motorcycle, so how bad could he be? Should I give it a try? If I didn't like it, I could always quit, right?

I got up. "I'll let you know. May I go now?"

"Sure. It's good to meet you."

I turned around at the door. "You know, my parents want me to go to boarding school, and I don't want to do it."

"Why not?"

"I'd probably mess up there too."

" 'Too'?"

"Just like here. My stupid sister gets to stay home, but they want to send me away. They're ashamed of me."

"Why do you say that?"

"I've given them lots of problems." I zipped up my jacket. "I'll call you."

On Seventy-second Street people were pouring out of the subway. I peered into their eyes as they passed. Had any of them ever seen a "shrink"?

Were other kids in therapy too? I stared at a guy, about my age, in a red shirt. I tried to send the message: "I'm a crazy patient, about to start therapy. Were you ever one?" But Red Shirt stopped to buy a candy bar at a newsstand. He gave some coins to the dealer, and ran across Broadway.

35

Caroline

You know those Greek comedy and tragedy masks —one smiling and one looking unhappy? You see them on theater programs and T-shirts?

Well, they were both Adam: grim face as he went to school in the morning, but in the afternoon, he'd swing laughing through the door—red in his cheeks, his hair flying around his head, his eyes sparkling.

"Boy, you're happy as a fig tree in Texas," Jo would say.

"Hi, there, gorgeous," he'd say and give her a big hug. "What can I eat?"

He'd be in the refrigerator, the TV would blast on, and he'd sing. He really does have a great voice. Even I have to admit it.

"Adam, you're too damn happy," Jo said.

"I feel great!"

"Your eyes could start a fire. You're on the junk."

That would stop him for a minute. "Oh, come on, Mrs. Smart, you're too serious. Can't we have a little fun?"

"Not when you're doped up, boy."

"Adam, why don't you admit it?" I'd ask. "Why don't you go to someone for help?"

"Caroline, get lost!"

He'd dance around the kitchen, but he'd keep moving and turning so that we couldn't see his face.

"You look at me!" Jo said. "I know you're smoking pot. What else are you doing?"

"Adam, listen to Jo!" I said. "She's trying to help you!"

He'd grab a piece of toast and say, "Catch!" He'd make Jo laugh and then they'd punch each other a little, like prizefighters.

"Josephine, I know you love me. And I love you too."

"Adam, one day your folks are going to come home early and smell that stuff. You'll be in deep trouble."

He'd start to waltz with her, kiss her cheek, hum a little tune. She'd put on a disgusted face, but then she'd start to hum, and they'd twirl around some more.

I stood there and watched them. How could Mom and Dad be so blind? Someone had to tell them.

36

Adam

THERE'S this great Cuban-Chinese restaurant on Seventy-eighth and Broadway where you can get a truckload of cheap, delicious food.

One Sunday night, when Mom was in a play and Caroline was sleeping over at a friend's house, Dad and I decided to go out to dinner.

We threw on our jackets and closed the front windows.

The Hudson River was blue and orange, the sky streaked with yellow.

"Hurry," said Dad. "We're going to miss the sunset."

"I'll turn on a lamp in the back 'for the burglars.' "

"We'll be back in a shake," Dad said. "Leave it!"

As the colors faded, a skinny moon came out. My dad put his arm around me, and we walked to the restaurant. It was nice to have him all to myself.

After dinner we wandered up Broadway.

"Adam, you've got homework?"

"Just math," I said.

"I've got to stop at the Korean market. Got your key?" I dangled it in the air and turned toward our apartment.

Hector, our elevator man, watched me cross the street, as if to keep evil spirits away. Maybe he watched me because I was so short and looked about ten instead of fourteen. To Hector, I was probably still the wrinkled baby who came home from the hospital in a blue basket.

I could see my face in the brass nameplate on our door as I unlocked the two double locks and pushed into the foyer. I threw my sneakers into the giant wicker basket and put the key onto the little chest.

I stopped. I had a funny feeling. It wasn't quiet enough, you know what I mean? Something was alive somewhere.

Had we left the radio on? I checked the hi-fi in the living room. No little red lights. Into the kitchen. The television on the counter was dark. Down the long hall and into my parents' room. Only the whirring noise of the battery clock.

Then I heard a scuffling, as if someone were trying to hide. Or two someones. My heartbeat flooded into my ears. I backed into the bathroom door.

124

More scuffling. A voice. Another voice. They knew someone else was in the apartment. Did they have guns? Knives?

I edged back toward the foyer, grabbed my key, and practically crawled to the elevator. I rang, but it didn't come.

I ran down to the superintendent's apartment and leaned against the bell. No answer.

I ran for the pay phone and dialed 911. The dispatcher told me to meet the cop car in front of the building.

I practically fell down the front steps into my father's arms. He dropped the grocery bag, and I blurted out the story. He started to tremble. When he's upset, his tremor gets worse.

When we entered the apartment with the police, it looked very peaceful. Nothing out of place. No broken glass or ransacked drawers. Was I nuts?

But Dad noticed my mother's jewelry chest was missing. And his cuff-link box. My calculator, the typewriter, and the electric razor were gone. So were Caroline's silver picture frames and fountain pens.

"Those guys knew this place," one of the cops said.

Dad and I looked at each other.

My throat closed, and my knees started to shake, so I sat down quickly, before anyone noticed.

"How did they get in and out?" I asked.

"The fire escape," said the other cop. He held up Caroline's wallet. "That's where we found this."

"But it's seven floors down to a cement court-yard," said Dad.

"They took the chance. The window was wide open. Were any lights on?"

This time Dad and I were afraid to look at each other. He grew pale, and the tremor made his hands jerk up and down. He sat down next to me.

"No," we said.

The cops, practically yawning, wrote down the details. "It happens hundreds of times a day," they said. "Not much hope of catching them, but we'll go through the fingerprint files and let you know if we find anything."

I stared down at the floor. I knew who these burglars were.

37

Adam

AT eleven that same night, Mom came home from her performance. It was the last one of the week, and she was smiling as she got off the elevator.

Dad and I met her in front of our door.

"Ann, darling, now don't panic, but I have something . . ."

I could feel myself shake as I stood behind him.

"Is someone hurt?" she asked. "Where's Caroline?"

"She's sleeping over at Sarah's," Dad said. "Did you have a good show?"

"Yes, thanks." She stared at us. "Jacob, please, what is it?"

I crept under Dad's arm. "We've been robbed,

Ann. Someone came through the fire-escape window."

Mom seemed paralyzed. "Were you hurt?"

"We're okay," said Dad.

"I heard them, Mom."

"Oh, God, you were here? You could have been killed!"

"No," Dad said. "He came in as they were probably going out the back. He ran down and called the police."

"What did they say?"

"The usual. They'll check back later. No clues, you know. Ann, dear, they took lots of things . . ."

"Who cares about 'things'?"

". . . all our small electronic stuff. Cassettes, radios, electric razors, calculators . . . anything they could get down the fire escape," said Dad. "And all your jewelry."

He steered Mom inside the apartment. We made tea. The steamy cup warmed my hands. We sat around the breakfast-room table and softly talked, as if someone had just died.

"Shall we call Caroline?" I asked.

"No need to spoil her evening," said Mom.

"We'll tell her in the morning," Dad said.

"Isn't it awful to think of the burglars touching our clothes, or clean linens, or going through the drawers?" asked Mom.

"It's over, now," Dad said. "Try not to think about it."

Later I couldn't fall asleep. My mother's sap-

128

phire engagement ring. Gone. Grandma's sterling silver, and Caroline's baby spoon and fork. My new radio and all my cassettes. Gone.

In the dark I shivered. I could hear Mom and Dad talking quietly in their room. Tomorrow Dad would order bars for the windows and new locks. But nothing would ever be the same again.

38

Caroline

JOSEPHINE was waiting for the elevator when I rushed home from Sarah's.

"Hi, hon. Why aren't you on your way to school?"

"I forgot my math book, and my report is in it!"

The elevator door clanked opened. Hector looked strange, nervous. Usually he and Josephine have this silly Spanish routine they go through every morning, but today he just took her umbrella and said, "They came in, Jo."

"Oh, my God, Hector . . . when?"

"Last night, around eight o'clock."

"Was anyone hurt?"

"No."

"Thank God."

"Who came in, Hector?" I asked. He just stared at me. "A friend of mine? Who . . . who came in?"

Jo put her arms around me. "He means robbers, hon, bad people came in."

My down jacket suddenly felt suffocating. I unzipped it.

"What did they take?" Jo asked.

"Small stuff. Mrs. Brody's jewelry. All the calculators, electric razors . . ."

"Razors? They'd risk their lives for a razor?"

"Yeah, and a couple of coats, and radios, cassettes. But too much for them to carry. They found things on the fire escape."

I had trouble catching my breath—the elevator was so hot!—and I leaned against the wall.

Hector steadied me with his hand. "Everyone's all right, Caroline. Don't be upset. They're upstairs."

"Did the police come?" Jo asked.

"Yes. They say it looks like an inside job. The burglars knew the place. You know who I think did it."

Hector and Jo exchanged a glance. "Yeah, I'm thinking the same thing," she said. "Those kids . . ." She stopped and looked at me. "But we got no proof, so we better not jump to . . ."

"What do you mean?" I asked. "Who do you think it was?"

"Now, cookie, we don't know," said Josephine. "There are crazy people out there on the streets."

But she signaled Hector with her eyes, and he turned away. No one said another word.

They thought it was one of Adam's awful friends! Someone who knew our house and went through all our things—my clothes, the desks and cabinets, the closets! Someone who'd been friendly with us and had stolen from us!

Josephine took off my jacket. "Okay, we're here," she said. "You're safe, Caroline."

But I was scared out of my mind. Which boy was it? I would never stay there alone—what if he came back? Our big, beautiful, sunny apartment! Someone had entered our house and hurt our lives!

How could we live here anymore?

39

Caroline

As usual, Adam got all the attention. Mom and Dad kept saying, "Oh, Adam, what if you had been hurt?" What about me? What if _I_ had walked into the apartment during the robbery? Lucky for them that I was at Sarah's—they didn't have to give me one thought. As usual. And then when I finally came home the next day, they just threw the news at me.

Everyone was so jittery, so I wanted to be calm about it. It's New York after all. People get robbed every day. What's the big deal? But then I discovered that my jewelry box had been taken. They took the whole box! My pearl earrings had been the best things I owned. And I got really angry. How dare someone take something I loved so much?

There were two men putting fancy gates on the windows, and the police came back and stayed two hours. Didn't they have anything else to do? They finally admitted they knew Mom from her sitcom on television and wanted her autograph!

Technically, they told us, we had been "burglarized," because we weren't at home when the "perpetrators" entered. It's called "robbery" when things are stolen while people are in the house. Either way it's a dreadful experience.

Adam sat in the living room most of that day. His weird friends didn't come over. Even Timothy Kim stayed away, which was too bad. He was the only one I could stand.

I had a lot on my mind too. This seems absurd, but I was beginning to realize that I'd never have good cheekbones. Or any cheekbones. I don't know why this bothered me so much. Mom has these great cheekbones, even though she's one of the oldest parents in my class. And it's embarrassing when all the other mothers wear wool skirts and tights, and Mom comes to school in her beaded and embroidered clothes with tons of bracelets and necklaces like some refugee from a gypsy camp. For some reason, I started getting angry about things like that.

After the burglary, things at home were pretty quiet. Adam tried to do his homework by himself, but halfway through, he'd lie down and go sound asleep. He'd have to be waked up to brush his teeth and get under the covers.

After Daddy switched off the brand-new electric typewriter, he'd bend over to kiss Adam. But Adam would just murmur a little and turn toward the wall, and Dad would stand there for a moment, looking unbelievably sad.

40

Adam

AFTER the burglary, I couldn't feel the same about my friends. I was pretty sure that Timothy had done it. He suddenly had hundreds of dollars.

He bought new boots and cassettes and a duffle coat and kept treating us all to pizza and Chinese food. He gave us tickets to rock concerts and ball games at the Meadowlands. I stopped accepting things. I mean, if the money came from our own stolen goods, it would have been pathetic.

"Where did you get all the dough?" I asked.

He looked away. "Oh, my father gave me birthday money."

Now Mr. Kim never gave him one cent. Sometimes, when he discovered cigarette papers and grass in Timothy's closet, he'd lock him out for days, without any money.

Tim had spent lots of time with us and knew every corner of our apartment. Once I'd found him in my mother's room.

"What are you doing in here?"

"I'm looking for the *TV Guide*," he said. Did he think I believed that?

But I had no proof. I wanted to tell Mom and Dad, but what if I was wrong? And I was afraid they'd realize I was smoking pot.

I didn't know what to do.

41

Caroline

It had been weeks since the burglary. Every few days Mom would say, "Oh, no! Those earrings! They took those too!" Or, "Has anyone seen my bracelet? Wait . . . I forgot . . ."

We'd all just stand there.

"I'm sorry," she'd say. "I know they're just 'things,' but when I start to get dressed . . ."

"You remember something else that's missing," said Dad.

"Exactly."

Adam would walk out of the room, and Mom would get busy cooking or exercising, but the shadows of those burglars still moved through the house.

Meanwhile Timothy had all these new clothes. He was tossing money around like mad, and those other boys weren't coming around anymore. Something was funny.

"Adam, did Timothy take our stuff?" I asked.

"Big mouth! What are you talking about?"

"He offered me tickets to the tennis matches at Madison Square Garden . . . where did he get money like that? And look at him—a new leather jacket!"

"Since when did you become Sherlock Holmes?"

But he was ferociously twisting a rubber band around his wrist. I sat down on his bed.

"Adam, if it's true, you have to tell Mom and Dad."

"They'll think I'm a crook *and* a dummy!"

I sighed. "Don't ever call yourself a dummy. You're not. Look, I know how hard everything is for you. I'm dyslexic too. You know that! Don't you think I get discouraged?"

"You're not as bad as I am."

"But I hate it as much as you do. And I'm not going to let it stop me."

"Oh, you're just a perfect person, Caroline."

"Well, you've got to find a way around it."

"Talk to me in about a year. I've got better things to do!"

He slammed the door as I walked out of his room. Soon the Rolling Stones were at thousand-decibel level. I stuffed cotton into my ears, but I couldn't concentrate. I sat down on the floor in the corner of my room and just stared.

If Mom and Dad knew about Timothy and the

drugs, they could help Adam. Jo thought he should confess by himself. She kept trying to tell him that.

Should I tell them? At least about the burglary? But then I remembered that demon psychologist, Dr. Martin.

Adam had enough bad stuff going on. I just couldn't add to it.

42

Adam

Ron Davis was always alone in his family's big brownstone. He'd chain the door of his room and close the windows.

We'd hug the huge plastic bags of marijuana like teddy bears. We'd share a joint and lay on the floor, listening to heavy metal.

"Didn't you have basketball practice today?" Ron asked.

"I'm off the team. Too short. Who cares? The school has crummy sports anyhow."

"Adam, wanna try some acid?"

"Why?"

"Oh, just for kicks. You'd love it, man."

"How much?"

"I'll bill you later."

Ron pulled a plastic zip-bag from his dresser. He held up a tiny square of paper.

"How do I do it?" I pretended to be casual, but this was a new ball game.

He held the paper with a pair of tweezers. "Now put this on your tongue."

"Maybe I should wait till I get home."

"Be cool. You won't feel anything for a while."

The paper dissolved in my mouth. Just disappeared.

"Okay," said Ron. "Go home and have a ball."

Up the street and into the lobby. Key in the front lock. Shoes off and into the straw basket. I felt perfectly normal.

"Adam, you look crazy." Josephine popped around the breakfast-room doorway.

"Crazy because I love you," I said. I tried to put my arms around her, but she jumped back.

"Boy, you smell like a bad hallway. Where you been?"

"I had basketball practice."

"You're lying. You're off the team. You told me."

"Big deal, Jo."

Down the long hall, the patterned wallpaper buzzing a little. Into my room. Books out, desk light on. Now I had to do my English.

I turned on my electric typewriter and rolled in a piece of paper. Nathaniel Hawthorne. *The Scarlet Letter*. The "Big A." Poor Hester Prynne.

Why was the air suddenly separating into little lines? And the lines turning into blocks? I was feeling so queasy. Better get food.

"Jo, what can I eat?" I leaned against the kitchen counter.

"I'm not talking to you when you're like that. Find your own food."

The crunch of apples hurt my ears. Back to the room. My eyes wouldn't focus. The air was splitting into dots and dashes again.

"Dinner, Adam." Dad was knocking on the door. Pause. "Are you all right?"

"I'm doing my homework."

"I called at five. You weren't home yet."

"I went to a friend's house." I opened the door. "Don't you trust me?"

"Of course, but we're not nuts about your riding the subway."

"Then why did you send me to a school practically at the Brooklyn Bridge?"

"Adam, lower your voice. What's eating you?"

"Nothing. I'm fourteen years old, and you want to follow me around. Leave me alone! I have work to do." I slammed the door.

I fell asleep around midnight, but I woke up at one, sweaty and panting. The headboard looked like a polar bear with shining, white teeth. Was this what acid did? I dozed.

Jerked awake again. The ceiling was falling in. I ducked my head. Under the pillow were circles of color, growing smaller, then larger. Bolts of light flashed on and off like neon signs. The walls were waves, foaming and breaking into spray. The bed was buckling. I held on tight.

I crawled across the room and grabbed some

143

notebook paper from the desk. Under the dresser—a red Magic Marker.

Sitting on the floor, I tore the paper into strips. By the light in the bathroom, I wrote, "I am dying!" Another strip of paper: "I'll commit suicide." Another piece of paper, now really small and ragged, "I have no life." Finally, "I can't read, I can't read, I can't read."

Lying back, I threw the papers into the air. They floated down like crackling snow.

Would I die now? Sleep was all I wanted. I shivered and half-covered myself with a blanket. The floor was cold.

I could hear the garbage trucks. It was morning. How would I get up for school? Or would I wake up at all?

Light came through the window blinds. A fire engine roared by. Finally—I don't know how—I slept.

43

Adam

DAD knocked on my door to wake me for school. I was too hung over to answer. He stepped into the room and stumbled over something on the floor, under the comforter. Me.

"My God, Adam! What's the matter? Why aren't you in bed? Are you sick?"

"Had a bad night, Dad."

Torn papers were scattered everywhere. He began gathering them.

"What are these?"

"Please don't look. _Please!_"

"What happened?"

"I can't talk about it." My teeth were chattering, and I tried to stand up. "I'm going to call Covan right away."

My knees buckled. Dad grabbed me and held me close.

"Adam, you're stoned!"

"I'm not!"

"We've suspected it for a long time."

"Who suspected it?"

"Josephine. We had a long talk this week."

"She's a rat."

"She loves you, Adam. We knew it too. We've been denying it this entire year. How much did you smoke last night?"

"I didn't. It was . . ."

"Tell me the truth."

"It was . . . LSD."

"Oh, Adam . . ."

I began to cry. "I was really scared, Daddy."

"Let's get you into the shower. I'll call the school."

"Okay. Thanks."

"This is your last day of using any sort of drugs. Do you understand? Your last day."

"Okay. Okay." I was sweating as I leaned against the bathroom sink.

"You could kill yourself this way, Adam."

"I know, Dad. I know."

44

Caroline

DAD and Mom were arguing in the hall while I sat in the breakfast room with my cereal. About five minutes later, Adam lurched into a chair, his hair still wet from the shower.

"What's going on?" I asked.

"I had a bad trip last night. Acid."

"Are you *crazy*?"

Mom sat down at the table. "Adam, I'm not going to be a nurse for the rest of my life." She was holding a cup of coffee and speaking very softly.

"We know you're suffering at school," said Dad, "but if you'd talk to us, we could help you."

"I'm sorry, I'm sorry!"

"They had to find out sooner or later," I said, pouring juice.

"Shut up, Caroline! You probably told too."

"I did not. *You* shut up!"

"Stop it!" said Mom. "Adam, Caroline did not tell on you. And you're starting a plan of recovery today!"

"And so are we," said Dad.

"Amen," said Jo.

"Thanks for squealing, Jo."

"You were sinking, boy!"

"And one more thing," said Mom. She was shouting now. "If you don't get over this, I'm not sure you can live here!"

Adam looked as if she'd hit him. Throw him out? Where would he go? What if he could never get better? Where was my little brother? For the first time I felt really frightened for him.

"Mom, wait a minute," I said.

"No more pot or acid or anything else!" Mom stood up. "Is that clear?"

"Yes! Stop screaming at me!"

"Adam, what time is Covan expecting you?" Dad asked.

"Ten o'clock."

"Get your coat. I'll drop you off."

"Thanks." Adam picked up his cap. Josephine started to put her arms around him, but he shoved her away.

I just stood very still. The door slammed behind Daddy and Adam. I could hear the clock chiming in the living room. There wasn't another sound anywhere.

45

Adam

"Am I completely crazy?"

Dr. Covan looked at my wrinkled, torn papers in his hands. "Absolutely not."

"But I wanted to be dead."

"We all have those thoughts. But you're here this morning."

"Yeah, but in heaven I might learn to read. Can't you see me spelling up there in the clouds?"

"Why don't we try planet Earth first?"

My mouth was wandering all over my face. I tried to make it into a normal shape, but it wasn't working. "I don't see any way out, Dr. Covan."

"Do you think drugs are going to help you find a way?"

"No, but they help me forget everything." I got

up from the chair and started marching around the room like a wind-up toy.

"Listen, Adam . . ."

"I'm a failure! Everyone hates me! Oh, God, I'm so thirsty."

"Okay. Sit still."

He went to the kitchen and brought back a glass of orange juice. He sat down, his cowboy boots half-disappearing into the shag rug.

"I hate shag rugs, Doc."

"Why?"

"I always think there are things crawling around in them."

"Like those things in your room last night?"

"Millions of 'em."

"There was nothing there, you know. It was the acid."

I took a long drink. "I suppose I could consider that dork school in New Jersey."

"Good idea."

"But they'll make me repeat the grade."

"It'd give you a chance to catch up, Adam."

"What if I bum out there?"

"What if you don't?"

He smiled at me. I felt like Frankenstein's monster slowly turning back into a human being.

"I've been inquiring about the Eckhardt School." Dr. Covan put his feet up on the hassock. "Their kids learn to read and go on to swell colleges."

"I won't wear a tie and jacket."

"Why don't you take another look?"

"Do you think it's my last chance?"

"No, but it's a good chance. You've got to get your life back, Adam."

I stood up. "Am I through?"

"You've got about fifteen more minutes."

"Listen, Doc . . ." I walked to the bookcase, my back to him. My throat felt like the California desert. I opened my mouth, and this squeak came out.

"Tell me," he said.

"What would you say if . . ."

". . . What?"

"I think I know who robbed us."

"Do you have proof?"

"This kid I hang out with has been loaded with money. He's been buying me tickets to concerts and movies and stuff."

"Do you accept the tickets?"

"I did at first, but I can't do it anymore."

"Why?"

"I feel so guilty."

"You didn't come in through the window. Someone else did."

"I've got to tell my folks."

"Good idea."

I leaned forward. "Do you think I'm doomed to be a bad guy forever?"

"You've never been a bad guy."

"You just want me to go to boarding school."

"Away from distractions here. I'm your friend, remember me?"

I had this heavy dent in my chest. It was my heart, beating like some wild thing. I looked at Dr. Covan. He gave me this giant bear hug, and my heart slowed down.

"You're doing great, Adam."

"Thanks, Doc."

I started home. I was going to tell Mom and Dad everything.

46

Adam

"WHAT if I told you the worst thing you ever heard?"

"I'm prepared for anything," Dad said.

"Even if it makes you hate me?"

"Impossible," said Mom. She put down the Sunday *Times* and took off her glasses.

"I think"—there was a clamp around my chest—"Timothy Kim was the burglar."

"What makes you think so?" asked Dad. He was very pale.

"Because he was always wandering around the apartment, and now he has too much money."

"Adam, this is a powerful accusation," said Dad. "You've got to have real proof, or you could damage a lot of people."

"You don't have to find someone to blame,"

said Mom. "The stolen things are gone. We're all okay. Now we just have to heal a bit."

"Mom, I'm not trying to blame someone. I really believe he did it. He seems to want me to know somehow."

"What do you mean?" asked Dad.

"He has all these new clothes, and he wants to buy presents for everyone, and pizza, and tickets to Madison Square Garden. I took the tickets at first, but now I just can't do it anymore. I feel like such a jerk. Caroline and Jo think he did it too. So does Hector."

"Does he still come up here?"

"Sometimes, Dad. But I try to keep him out."

"Adam, I don't want him here!"

"Okay, Mom. I promise. Do you hate me now?"

"It wasn't your fault," Dad said.

"Yes, it was. I let those guys into the house."

Dad walked to the window. "Why have you been carrying this around? Why didn't you tell us?"

"I thought you'd kick me out."

"We let Timothy live here," Mom said. "How could he . . . ? Jay, can you talk to his father?"

"We have to prove this, Ann, but I'm going to do something."

"I wish I could take back everything I did," I said.

"What about telling the police, Jay?"

"Only if we're absolutely sure," said Dad.

"Adam, it's good you're being honest with us," said Mom.

"I'm so sorry about your jewelry—"

"It was terrible, those boys coming into this house. It makes me feel—"

"Mom, I know."

"I don't know what to say about this—"

"And there's something else."

"What?" Dad asked.

"I think I'd like to try the Eckhardt School."

Dad looked completely shocked. "Say that again, please?"

"I'd like to start over. I've got to read. I can't stand not being able to read! Being Adam Zigzag!"

"What?" asked Dad.

"Sometimes I call myself . . . Adam Zigzag . . ."

"Why on earth?" asked Mom.

". . . because everything I write looks nutty and squiggly. And my brain feels like that too."

"Well, you're Adam Brody, who's as smart as paint. A wonderful kid with lovely talents," said Mom. "There's nobody here named Zigzag."

"But that's not how I feel."

"I understand," said Dad, "but once you go away to school, that may all change."

"Can we afford boarding school?"

"We'll find a way," said Dad.

I stood there for a moment. No one spoke.

Finally Dad said, "It'll be a new beginning for us all."

Mom sighed. "Amen."

"Ditto," I said.

47

Adam

I WAS a dropout. One of those kids you read about in newspaper articles.

I had been accepted at Eckhardt, but they were going to make me repeat the grade when school began in September.

"Dad, I should quit school. I'm going to waste time these next three months."

"You can't just stay home."

"I'll get a job. What if I could work out a plan?"

"Adam, that's absurd," said Mom. "Not going to school is against the law, by the way."

But I went to the principal, Mr. White, at Amy Evans, and after about a thousand phone calls between the two schools and three meetings with my protesting parents, everyone agreed.

These were the conditions: I had to read books from a long list that Eckhardt gave me, I had to keep a journal, and I had to write a weekly letter to Mrs. Becker, my new principal.

This was a good deal! I was worried that I wouldn't be able to finish the reading, but in March I left Amy Evans and got a job scooping ice cream.

Every morning at eight I arrived at Deli Delight Ice Cream on Columbus Avenue. I mopped the floors, prepared the ice cream holders, arranged the chairs and tables, and started the soft-yogurt makers.

At first I loved it. I was earning money, and I didn't have to face teachers who had given up on me. Or do work that didn't make any sense. And after school, my friends dropped by. Oh, the free scoops I gave! I never knew I had so many friends! After two weeks, my scooping wrist was killing me.

The journal was actually a good thing. Nobody was grading my spelling, and I could let it all hang out. I could fill a page quickly with all kinds of things: about the job, about girls I wanted to date, my family, my fantasies. How sometimes I just wanted to get lost in the smoke of a big doobie, but I knew I couldn't. Sometimes I'd have really sweaty nightmares and wake up saying, "No! No! No!"

I discovered that withdrawing from drugs made me face all my fears—all those feelings of being no good and stupid and useless. (Here comes "Adam Zigzag!") Being scared was rough, but after a while I realized that it wasn't terminal. It didn't kill me. I wrote it all down and spewed it all out to Dr. Covan twice a week. He was great.

And I worked on the reading list. I could only read a few pages before I fell into a dead sleep, but gradually I stopped having a heart attack every time I opened a book.

One night I wrote this in my journal: "There is something about puting t~~ogithr~~ together words, that I love. Even in my broken-stik handwritin. I think I can realy do something with my life. Im not hopeless, but I need an e~~ducasion~~ educatin. Maybe boarding scool will be my last chance dress code and all. And I'll never agin have to where a white cap and say, 'Would you like a taste of today's flavir?' over and over and over."

48

Adam

AT first, Eckhardt was like a bad English movie. Strict, cold, full of rules, every minute scheduled. But I wasn't homesick at all! And I began to like wearing a shirt and tie.

My roommate's parents were divorced, and he didn't know where he belonged. He didn't really have a home. I felt sorry for him, but hey! I didn't know where I belonged either, so we kind of clung together.

The food was strangely okay. Dinners were worse than the other meals, but we survived. Boxes from home were godsends, and then we all pigged out.

The boarding school kids were from all over the world, even China and India. There were twin girls from Japan and a tribal prince from Africa! They were in the "English as a Second Language" program.

I had found a terrific school with good people. What if my parents couldn't have afforded it? Some of the students were on scholarship, and they had no spending money. It made me feel privileged and guilty, all at the same time. Mom and Dad had to work hard to keep me there, and I tried to hold down the small expenses—phone calls, dates on the weekend. I did pretty well except when the evening meal was slush, and we all sent out for pizza. To save our lives!

The students in the "Learning Skills" program were treated just like everyone else. It was even kind of an honor to be picked for it. For the first time in my life, I wasn't the only person who was having trouble. And I could breathe in class. I wasn't always afraid.

On the first day my Learning Skills teacher, Mrs. Kirschner, said, "You've devoted a lot of energy to *not* trying in school, haven't you?"

I stared at her. She had an X-ray mind. "I don't know."

"I think so, Adam. It's a natural response. Would you like a way to remember things?"

"I could remember things if I tried, but I don't want to."

"Sometimes we forget facts because we're concentrating so much on technical skills."

"You mean, reading and writing?"

"Yes, and getting the numbers down neatly—things that take so much time. I'm going to teach you to use the computer. It'll do a lot of the work automatically. Save you hours."

"What if nothing works?"

"Then we'll revise our plans. We're going to make up a program just for you, to serve your needs. Would you like that?"

"I think so."

"We have high expectations for you. You're going to have to work hard. I know you're ready, or you wouldn't be here."

"It's because my parents want me here."

Mrs. Kirschner smiled. "Tell me what was hard for you at the other schools."

"Everything would have been easy. I told you, I just didn't want to do it."

"Aw, come on, Adam, tell me just one thing you did try to do, and it didn't work."

Long pause. Was she really on my side?

"Well, just one thing. It's hard for me to write."

"Physically hard?"

"Yes, it cramps my hand."

"What was easier for you?"

"Math sometimes. Sports. Language is a bust."

"It is for LD kids."

"Is that what I am . . . an 'LD kid'?"

"Yes, it's just a handy term for 'learning-disabled,' but I've got some ideas from the tests you took last week."

"You do?"

"I have a hunch you're going to be good in language and reading. Especially writing. We'll see. What sports are you going out for?"

"Tennis."

"Perfect. Tonight you'll work on this Shirley Jackson story called 'The Lottery,' and I want a report in the morning."

"What?"

"We work from day one, Adam. You're going to have to do what you hate to do . . . every day . . . and you're going to be graded on it."

I groaned.

"It's not so bad. The grades will be subjective. We take into consideration your effort and your personal progress. That's pretty fair, isn't it?"

"But I hate book reports."

"I'm going to help you get started. Here's your assignment book."

"My what?"

"Your very own, individualized assignment book. Write down each class assignment, and check them off as they're finished."

"Mrs. Kirschner, I can't do all that."

"Of course you can. I'll teach you how to take efficient class notes."

"And then what?"

"Perhaps you'll put them on tape and listen to them. Or maybe, in your room, you'll write each note one extra time and then work from that set."

"This is too much!"

"Not at all. Tomorrow bring in the Jackson report. Do it in longhand for now. You'll be at your desk each night from seven to ten o'clock, so you'll have plenty of time."

"Is it true we can't make phone calls or play music then?"

"Or *receive* phone calls, or eat, or visit, or sleep, or go to the vending machines."

"I'm gonna die."

"You're going to love it. And by the way, I'm always here. Not only in our sessions, but all day long, after school, at home . . . here's the number. Call on me anytime."

"Thanks." I was losing the war. "Anything else?"

"Just . . . good luck, Adam. We're awfully glad to have you here."

The word processor is the greatest machine ever invented! I could *write*! I could express my thoughts! I could fool around with the sentences until they were perfect. And there was a disc to correct my spelling. A miracle!

I learned to follow lines down the pages of books. That white space in the middle didn't appear so often, but if it did, Mrs. K. showed me how to get back my place without panicking. She taught me to organize my homework, take notes, and use the library.

Next to Dr. Covan, I'd never had a friend I could tell everything to. Mrs. Kirschner knew I had been on drugs, and we talked about it a lot. There was stuff available at school—no big secret—but if I started smoking again, she would be so disappointed in me. And I'd hate myself.

At the end of the first term, I wrote this essay:

"My name is Adam Brody, and I am dyslexic. I have trouble arranging words and organizing my thoughts. When I was little, my handwriting was so bad that I called myself 'Adam Zigzag.' I was tested for dyslexia when I was seven years old. Even though I have gone through many tests and tutors, I still have trouble and wonder if I always will.

"From the fourth or fifth grade until now, I have spent at least two hours a week in different tutors' homes and offices. I hated to go. Another awful part about being dyslexic was having to go to hospitals and places where I felt like I had something wrong with me.

"Sometimes when I think about all the money and time my parents have spent on me while I was jerking-off in classes at school, I could just shoot myself. I wonder: did any of the time I spent with previous tutors pay off?

"Will I ever really get over dyslexia? Being dyslexic has put voices inside my head that keep on telling me that I can't make it, or that I am not as good as someone else. I sometimes think that people don't like me or that I won't be accepted. Another bad part of dyslexia is the mental part, which is what might stay with me for a long time. It will be very hard to fight this disease."

49

Caroline

WHEN Adam left for boarding school, the apartment was strangely quiet.

No dope smokers slammed in and out of the refrigerator. No rock music. No arguments between Adam and Mom, and Daddy began to lose that worry line above his glasses.

The bathroom stayed neat. The grungy toothpaste tube wasn't stuck behind the wastebasket, and jackets and shoes weren't scattered over the floor of the foyer.

When twelfth grade began, I was still feeling a little down about not getting into Darby. But now when the phone rang, it was for me. Friends came to visit. I could have lots of girls to sleep over. Some in my room, some in Adam's.

Josephine missed him. She was always cleaning his room, changing the sheets, polishing his desk. As if he were there. Once she just leaned against his door and cried.

"Jo, he'll be back for Thanksgiving," I said.

"How you think he's doing?"

"Well, no one's called to complain about him. And he says he loves it."

"Oh, girl, maybe that place is what he's been looking for."

Most nights I did my homework. For once my mother wasn't in a play or in California, and she and Daddy listened to music and read in the living room.

Sometimes they took me to restaurants and movies, or to the theater. I'd sit between them, their shoulders touching mine. Mom would hold my hand, and Daddy would put his arm around me. I'd wake him up if he dozed off, and he'd whisper, "Thanks, honey." I felt like a little girl again.

They helped me with college applications and talked about their universities.

"In the olden days?" I'd ask.

Daddy laughed. "In the *very* olden days."

There seemed to be a new kind of rhythm in the house. Calmer. Slower. But we would never be the same. Adam had brought the outside, dangerous world into our house. He had lied until he couldn't lie anymore, and although no one said it, we all felt damaged.

Mom and Dad were trying to make up for all

the time they had concentrated on Adam. But they still jumped when the phone rang, and their eyes were filled with thoughts of love. For me, of course. But mostly, for him.

I didn't miss him. I thought I should, but I didn't miss him at all.

50

Adam

I⊤ was not absolutely perfect at Eckhardt. There was no drama department. There was this excellent teacher, Mr. Evans, who directed plays after school, but we had to give up the auditorium to some other group at least twice a week.

The first semester I did a small part in _Inherit the Wind_. It was fun! It was as if I had come home to a familiar, happy country.

Then I made the tennis team, but I still had to take Physical Education every day. I didn't have time to do it all. I asked for an appointment with the headmaster.

His office was full of polished antiques and a fat red-leather sofa. And pictures of dogs and horses in gold frames. Dogs in paintings always look as if they're stuffed, their eyes kind of popped open and their paws planted in some dead position on a velvet pillow.

"Dr. Duncan, I'd like to use the tennis team as my Physical Education requirement."

"No, Adam. Tennis and drama are extracurricular activities. Physical Education grades are needed for college."

"Yes, sir, but we practice every day for two hours. I get a better workout there than I would in the gym."

"You'll have to make the choice, Adam."

"Well, sir, if I could use gym period as study hall, I could practice tennis and still rehearse until right before dinner."

"And what about the requirements for graduation?"

"Dr. Duncan, I'll be representing the school in all the tennis meets. Shouldn't that count as a requirement?"

This stopped him for a minute. I couldn't believe I was in this situation. I had never stood up for myself. My mother and father had always had to do it.

"You have to take P.E., that's all. Perhaps you'd better give up theater activities and go with the tennis."

"No, sir, I can't do that." Was this me talking? "Tennis means everything to me, but I might want to be an actor. I need the experience now."

"We're not here to train actors."

"Excuse me, sir, but do you think you could just consider this? It means a lot to me."

"I'll talk to Mrs. Kirschner and your teachers, but I don't hold out any hope, Adam."

As I bent to pick up my bag, I noticed the oriental carpet. Designed by some artist in Iran or India or some other far-off country, who probably sat cross-legged for a million hours, with babies crawling around and a smoky fire to warm the tent. How could Dr. Duncan live with this amazing design and think that an art like theater wasn't important?

Didn't he know that kids needed other stuff besides books and classes? It was time to change the old-fashioned attitudes of the Eckhardt School. It wasn't going to be easy, but I was going to do it.

51

Adam

Dear Mom and Dad:

I hope you enjoyed my last letter. I received both of yours and loved them. This experience at Eckhardt is intense. The computer is intense. I can't stop using it. You were really great to give it to me, as I know it must have cost a bundle.

Please give my love to Josephine and Caroline. Hope you are all coming up for the tennis match.

so how's life? I only ranked 40 out of 98 in my class. I was pretty upset, but Mrs. Kirschner (my Learning Skills teacher) said that I should be happy. I don't want you and Dad to think that I'm waisting your money. I try hard, but it's especially hard to do hard work when you are unselfish.

(Just kidding)

I love you.

Adam

P.S. Write back

52

Caroline

CHRISTMAS lights and oversized tinsel waved in the cold wind on the highway to Princeton. We were on our way to see Adam's sophomore class play.

I was driving our car. At the University of Southern California, where I was a freshman, everyone drives, and Dad and Mom had bought me a secondhand car. Out there I was independent! I could go anywhere, anytime! The palm trees and the mountains and the smog whizzed by, and I felt like a real grown-up.

And I loved the university. I was studying theater and French and art history and English literature. I wore shorts and a T-shirt to class. I could choose my own meals. It seemed like the beginning of my life. Finally.

Now I was home for the winter holidays. Mom sat in the backseat.

"Caroline, there's a stop sign coming up." She was hissing through her teeth, the way she always does when she gets nervous.

"Mom, I'm a very good driver."

"She really is, Ann. Relax," Daddy said.

Adam and his teacher, Mr. Evans, had persuaded the headmaster to let them do *On the Razzle*, by Tom Stoppard, a way-out choice for that proper school. Adam had shaken up things around there: They had a real drama program for the first time, and everyone was excited about it.

The auditorium was so full that people stood against the walls, and some of the younger students sat on the floor in front. The snow began to flick against the windows. It was delicate and sparkly, like the fake glitter that comes in a bag.

When the curtain went up, Mom looked as if she were in the center of a tiny, fierce hurricane, her eyes glued to Adam. She clutched the arms of her seat. A film of perspiration covered Dad's forehead.

"He's talented," Dad whispered. "And he seems confident. What a change in one year!" Mom nodded and, for a moment, leaned her head on Dad's shoulder.

Adam really was amazing. He seemed to be part of the stage, as if he lived there. He was having fun. The audience yelled and applauded all through the evening. It was a funny, crazy production.

I was jealous. Absolutely. Once again, he was

the center of attention. (What else was new?) But I knew how far he had come. How his life had almost slipped away. And now he could read and write and act!

Then there were eleven curtain calls, and then it was over.

"How did you like it?" asked Adam, rushing out to join us. "Can we eat now? What did you think of the direction?"

"Congratulations, Adam," said Daddy. "Are you too old and successful for a hug?"

"No, gosh . . . no, Dad. Thanks for coming. Did you like it? Isn't Paul Kahn a great actor? How was the trip down? Want Mexican food? It's the only decent place open late. Everything else sucks. Oh, except for the Buffalo wings joint . . . want to go there?"

We walked across the midway with all the other actors and the audience. A dome of stars shot speckled light down onto the enormous snowy pine trees. Music trickled from the dormitory windows.

"Your acting was fantastic," Dad said, as we all arranged ourselves in the car.

"Simple, real, unpushy," said Mom. "Lovely detail."

"Gee, guys . . . thanks." Adam pointed the way to the restaurant. "And what do you think, Miss College Girl?" he asked.

"I hate to say it, but you were fabulous. You were the best one, by far."

"Do you mean it?" He was looking at me with

such love that I felt myself crumple into little pieces.

"Yes, I mean it. I hate to admit it, but I think you're on your way."

"You don't have to cross me at the stop lights anymore?"

"You remember that? You'd say we can't go 'too thoon. It would be dangerouth.' "

"I did not."

"You did!"

"How gross!"

"No, you were cute. And now you don't lisp. You're even getting decent-looking."

"Caroline," Daddy said. "Give the guy a break!"

"Yeah, Caroline, it would be none 'too thoon.' "

Dad started the car, and we turned onto the narrow road. The windows in the beautiful old Princeton houses made lighted picture frames in the night. In one a family was sitting around a table. In another a glass lamp sent colored reflections onto the white lawn. A woman holding a baby was lowering the shade in a living room.

We passed a clapboard house with a Christmas tree on the porch.

"You always wanted to live in a house like that, Caroline," Adam said.

"I know. I thought our lives would be perfect if we had a stairway to the bedrooms, and gardens and a swing."

"And rag rugs and cotton curtains," said Adam.

"Right. You remember that too!"

"No one's life is perfect," said Dad.

"Ours is," Adam said.

"Oh yeah, oh yeah?" I said. We all laughed, and Adam put his arms on the top of the front seat.

"Well, it's getting better, isn't it?" he asked.

"I'll say," said Mom.

"A thousand times better," I said. Adam leaned back and grinned at me.

The restaurant was crowded and steamy. Everyone sang along with the Christmas carols playing on the loudspeakers. And the Buffalo wings were the best I ever tasted.

53

Adam

At the end of my junior year, I read *Night*, by Elie Wiesel. About this kid surviving the Nazis and World War II by himself. He lost his family and friends and everything. I had never responded so emotionally to any other book.

The first thing I did after finishing the book was to call my father. I told him that he was the best father in the world.

"Dad, I've caused you a lot of pain."

"Not pain, Adam," he said. "Just concern that you would come through everything."

"Daddy, I'm sorry I didn't appreciate you every day."

"You did appreciate me, even if you weren't aware of it."

"I love you, Dad."

"I love you too, darling."

Here are the first paragraphs of my paper on *Night*.

"One morning I woke at nine-thirty and read *Night* until noon. It's a very short book, and I was reading faster than I ever had before.

"Hunger was the only reason I had for getting up. I was very hungry but I couldn't eat. I didn't deserve to eat. I sat in front of this plastic bowl of cold pasta I had made the night before and felt sick. What to do!

"After a long deliberation I put a piece of the ziti in my mouth and chewed it as if it were my last meal, concentrating on how lucky I was. Afterwards I got back in bed. Who was I to be so fortunate? The sheets were softer than I had remembered."

Then I wrote five pages about the book.
I got an A+. The first ever.

54

Adam

Dear Mom and Dad:

We're studying about John Lomax, who traveled the United States, recording old American ballads and interviewing the people who still sing them.

He must have loved his life, discovering little towns tucked away in the Ozark Mountains and in Adirondack ravines. Singing folk songs around a campfire or on someone's front porch. Yesterday I played some of that music on my guitar!

This'll sound corny, but I'd like to make a contribution to the world. Like

John Lomax. Maybe be a writer or a psychologist or a musician. Don't laugh. I think I can do it, thanks to this school. And to you.

The graduation gowns and caps are red! They're going to look wild under the trees at the ceremony.

And, Mom, please don't be offended, but would you wear "Mother clothes"? Not your ethnic stuff with all the mixed-up patterns and bracelets? You know I love it, but they don't understand it down here. Thanks. I appreciate it a lot.

Tell Caroline and Josephine that I'm really glad they're coming to graduation. By the way, I made MVP (Most Valuable Player) on the tennis team this year. You'll see me get the award. What a blast!

I still can't believe I got into Syracuse and Ithaca College! Two schools. I'm in a state of shock! We have to talk!

I guess that's the end of "Adam Zigzag."

I'm now going to run my speller disc through the computer, and when you get this letter, it will be perfect.

I hope.

Love,

Adam

BARBARA BARRIE, an actress as well as an author, has appeared in numerous plays, films, and television shows. She has received Drama Desk and Obie awards and was nominated for an Oscar for her role as the mother in *Breaking Away* and a Tony Award for her work in the musical *Company*. She won Best Actress at the Cannes Film Festival for the groundbreaking film *One Potato, Two Potato*. She earned Emmy nominations for her roles in the television series *Breaking Away* and *Law and Order*. For many years she played Mrs. Miller on the series *Barney Miller*.

Barbara Barrie graduated from the University of Texas with a BFA in Drama. She lives in New York City with her husband, Jay Harnick, a producer and director. Their children, Jane and Aaron, are both writers and actors.

She is the author of *Lone Star*, a novel based on her screenplay, *The Chanukah Bush*.